BROKEN TRUST

Thomas Habersham

Contact Author:
Thomashabersham844@gmail.com

Contact TMA Publishing:
tmapublishing@yahoo.com

ISBN: 978-0-615-99540-3

ISBN-13: 978-0-615-99540-3

WORDS FROM THE AUTHOR

I once shared a manuscript with a friend who found it intriguing enough to share it with another. He returned and informed me as to what he'd done, quoting the other's sentiments regarding my work. Publishing, then, was only a dream. With that, I knew mixed emotions at the words spoken to me.

"He said you didn't write this," my friend confided. "He said you must have copied it from somewhere, because if you were that good, you'd be published."

Well… The manuscript in question is the one before you.

DEDICATION

Behind me– and everything you see –there is a spectacular woman; her name is Stephanie.

Chapter 1

Ashley Rowan lay in bed fearfully awaiting the inevitable. She glanced at the bedside clock: 2:03 a.m.

He was late, she thought. Maybe he wouldn't come home tonight. With her luck, fate wouldn't be so kind; he would show for certain, to inflict pain, to torture.

"Please, Lord," Ashley prayed aloud for the umpteenth time within the last hour. "Can I have one night alone?" Her prayers to God were less frequent of late, her faith having fallen near the wayside. She called to him this night, however, as she had many times before, seeking refuge from the tormenting hand of torture.

The distant slam of the front door resounded throughout the house.

"God, please!" Ashley pleaded with all her heart, willing her Father to oblige. She once knew serenity in coming to the Lord and having offered her burden in prayer, but there was only fear now; a wrenched gut and a quickened pulse.

Although her room door was shut, locked from the outside, the house was quiet and his heavy tread echoed up the empty hall, slow, deliberate, and tantalizing. A terror inducing tact, she recognized, and he took pleasure in the act. Of this she was certain.

His tread became silent, strumming the chords of agonizing suspense. Would he retire to his own room, sparing her a night's torment, or would he barge in and do to her what normal men did not do to women? The suspense was strategically drawn out at times, boosting her terror to incapacitating height.

There came the faint but unmistakable scrape of the key sliding into the lock, pins clicking into place, and the thud of a thrown bolt. Terror-enhanced, the noise was ominous, and the door swinging open with James' menacing figure silhouetted against the hall's light was foreboding. He was big, standing six-two and weighing two-hundred-twenty pounds. In spite of his intimidating physique, his boyishly handsome face portrayed innocence, that which had persuaded her to represent him. She had gotten him off of the criminal charges, but it had been a terrible mistake.

James Lynn had been charged with two counts of rape and aggravated sexual battery. He'd hired Ashley as his attorney in going to trial with the aim for acquittal. He had known well the advantage of female representation considering the charges. The evidence presented was overbearing at times, and Ashley had reservations regarding their success, but the ruling was in their favor; he had been acquitted.

Total strangers at first, their relationship had been nothing other than professional. After multiple meetings and over the course of the trial, Ashley became somewhat fond of him, accepting the proposed invitation to dinner upon their victory. Having had a few drinks, and conversation on a more personal level, James extended his invitation further in suggesting Ashley accompany him to his bedroom. She politely declined, reminding him of her engagement and coming marriage.

Ashley left North Carolina for her home in Georgia, thereafter maintaining contact with James via email and text. In two months her curiosity was piqued; she wanted to sample sex with James, and she made preparations for the trip, fabricating a tale of having been retained once again in the state of North Carolina.

"It seems my angel is making a name for herself." Her fiancé, Trayon, had kissed her pridefully.

"Looks that way," she said, pressing close to him. Though success was still hers to obtain, Trayon had provided the opportunity of pursuit.

Her intent had been to sleep once with James and return to Trayon, but fate hadn't been so kind. The sex was addictive and she couldn't stop. Her indulgence was fierce, repetitive until the moment she called home and was denounced by her fiancé. The conversation was as fresh to her now as it had been five months ago.

"Hello?" Trayon had answered midways through the second ring.

"Hey," Ashley greeted. "How are you?"

"Distracted, and I can't get anywhere with the manuscript."

"I'm sorry, baby. All is well on my end."

''You've won the trial?" he asked.

"Not yet. It'll be over tomorrow, but it's definitely in my favor. I'll be on the first flight home afterwards. I can't wait to see you."

He made no comment.

"Don't you miss me?" she asked teasingly.

Silence.

Apprehension began to creep. "You there, honey?"

"Yeah," came his curt reply.

"Are you feeling okay, Trayon? You don't sound so well."

"Let me ask you something, Ashley," he said. "I need you to be honest with me."

"Aren't I always?" She laughed and hoped he couldn't detect the nervous tenor therein.

"Was there anything you ever wanted that I did not get for you?" he asked.

"No."

"Have you ever known distress at my hand?"

Her stomach tightened. "Why are—?"

"Just answer the question," he said.

"No I haven't." Her tone was defensive.

"Are you unhappy with me, Ashley?" His voice was strained. "Were you ever?"

"Baby no," she moaned, her answer and denial, knowing where this was headed.

"Is my sex good to you?" he went on.

"Yes."

"Is it good enough?"

"Of course it is, baby."

He breathed deeply and was silent for a second.

"Ashley, sweetie, if all is true, you have no reason to cheat on me."

"Cheat on you!" she exclaimed. "I would never cheat on you! Is this some kind of joke?"

"It's no joke, and you know it."

Ashley was taken aback. What justified his allegation? "I don't know anything," she came back. "Why are you coming at me like that? Don't you trust me?"

He exhaled into the phone. "That was my mistake. I trusted you the way I trusted no one else. What is your excuse?"

"You can't be serious," she replied.

"Very stubborn," he said. "You make the perfect lawyer. Deny all you want but you're as guilty as Eve for biting the apple and coaxing Adam."

She'd hurt him, and his voice carried the depth of his pain. She knew agony at having brought such to him, for it hadn't been her intent. His words were daggers to the heart. That she was guilty is true, but confess she could not. "That's enough," she said. "You've played this game long enough, and–"

"Cut the bullshit, Ashley!" he shouted into her ear. "We both know you're fucking a former client!"

Her fiancé was a man of God. That he shouted obscenities said much for his state regarding the matter. She felt an overwhelming desire to rectify her behavior and mend his heart, but how could she? "I'll be home tomorrow," she told him. "And if you really want to have this conversation, we will talk some more–"

"No," he said. "You are never to set foot in my house. I hope you earn enough in your new career to take care of yourself.

The line went silent.

"I was your miracle," his voice filled the silence. "I made it happen for you. You'll be sorry for this. Good-bye Ashley."

"Wait!" she started. "Tray, please, I lo–"

"I dare you!" he cut her off. "After all this, can you really say it? Can you really say you love me? I hope you're happy with your decision."

Now, almost six months later and the question still remains: how had he known?

"Are you angry I'm late?" James asked. He closed and locked the door behind him, approaching the bedside, unbuttoning his shirt.

Ashley clutched the bedcovers close to her chin. The question required no answer, so none was given. The desired effect, however, is what he saw reflected in her clear brown eyes. She was afraid of him, as he wanted her to be, terrified of what he may or may not visit upon her.

James flung the covers away and frowned at her T-shirt and panties, uttering his displeasure with such. "Why aren't you naked?"

Ashley cringed at his rising voice, not so much physical as it was mental. "My− I'm still on my period," she blurted. His eyes glinted, and she regretted her vain attempt. He would hurt her for certain.

"I know your cycle." He bent quickly, and just as fast, her arms came up defensively.

"Put down your arms!" he commanded. She did and he tore her T-shirt and panties away, leaving her naked and tense beneath his penetrating gaze. Her skin was caramel in color, a tone which sat well with her light color eyes. Her breast, twin peaks of perfection, were tipped with dark circles of cocoa.

Ashley knew well her attributes, the desire men harbored for a body such as her own. With her fiancé, she'd been continuously reminded of the beauty she possessed with his constant want for intimacy, their years together having no diminishing effect. She'd felt powerful with what she had on him, knowing bliss at his desire for her.

Earlier on, though not as intense, she'd known something similar with James. She loathed his arousal now, detested it with every fiber of her being. There was neither bliss nor power with him, only trepidation and terror.

He looked her over now, his gaze lingering at the mound of flesh peeking from beneath the dark springy curls between shapely thighs. He kicked off his shoes and unfastened his pants. "I was going to be lenient," he said. "Since you haven't learned to be honest... Well, you know the rest."

He stared as his pants fell to his ankles. She stared back; she did know, and there would be nothing to enjoy. Mercy would not come at her plea. It got her nowhere with him. Her heart pounded, and she could hear its thunderous beat. He seemed to thrive off her fear, and she desperately wanted to conceal it but couldn't; her terror was like that of a rabbit caught in the fox's shadow. Tears fell down her face. How had such a monster gotten ahold of her?

James kicked casually out of his boxers– then struck out lightning quick with a numbing backhand across Ashley's face. She cried out with as much surprise as pain, caught off guard by his swift attack. Tears flowed freely.

James pounced, using his knees to wedge open her legs, a gesture which met no resistance.

"I'm sorry," she cried. "It won't happen again."

"A little too late for that, don't you think?" He slapped her again, with his palm. Her head whiplashed and she cried out. "What's wrong?" he chided, staring into her fear-filled eyes. "Don't you like pain?" His excitement grew hard against her and she had the urge to slide away, but it would be an open act of rebellion, further invoking his wrath.

He stroked her face with his thumb. "You must like it," he said. "Why then do you play games with me?" He kissed her. She wrapped her arms around him and returned the kiss. Her response was not desire, but imposed conditions instead; it earned leniency.

"Spread your legs," he instructed, and she did un-hesitantly, adding with it a caress along his shoulders. "Good girl," he commented. "You keep that up and I may forget your deception."

"Please." She would like nothing better. But what will it be?

He smiled crookedly, guided his swollen member to her entrance, cuffed her buttocks– and rammed in forcefully, eliciting an agonizing wail. No matter her pretense, she wasn't ready– could hardly remember the last time she was ever –and such a ramrod entrance was excruciating. He pulled back and rammed in with even greater force, tearing at her insides. Again she screamed, digging her nails deep into his back. She did so in pain and out of anger. It was her only avenue to vent, the only retaliation for which he would not seek retribution, for it conveyed her suffering, distress, and the fact she detested what he visited upon her.

Long ago, just before one of his nightly visits, she'd taken the liberty of lubricating herself with Baby Oil. He'd entered her, had become instantly enraged, and had beaten her severely. That he wanted her to suffer his advance in its entirety, was clear. Although he'd never forbidden her against it, she understood the consequence and has never since bothered with lubrication, and now she suffered his torturous advance.

Her discomfort heightened his excitement to a level where he was done in minutes. It seemed an eternity of suffering, however; she couldn't wait for its end. She squirmed to reduce the force of his thrust. He hooked his arms behind her shoulders in response, pulling her to with every stroke. There was to be neither escape nor reprieve.

James paused momentarily and signaled Ashley with a hand to her thigh. Understanding clearly his desire, she lifted her legs and allowed them to be placed upon his shoulders, one to either side of his head. It would be even more severe. He resumed with a motion, almost gentle, but Ashley knew it wouldn't remain so. He would find a rhythm and fall to merciless hammering. The respite, however, was enough for her to adjust mentally, to become oblivious to pain.

With that, Ashley focused her mind on a time before her encounter with James. A time when she was well treated and loved. A time when she wasn't controlled but had free rein to do whatever, whenever. A time when she was deliriously happy in the arms of her fiancé; a time forever lost to her except in memory.

Following that surprising dismissal over the phone, Ashley had taken James as immediate replacement. After all, he'd been attempting for some time to coax her away from her fiancé, promising to keep her physically and emotionally sound. Moreover, he held the renowned status of an artist; she would never want for anything. All would be well, he'd promised, and well it had been for a time.

The conflict began one night after their return home from a dinner outing, the food having upset Ashley's stomach. James had wanted sex, and she could not oblige him. Unwilling to accept her dissent, their relationship took a turn for the worse. He raped her that night and every other thereafter, increasingly violent in every episode. She was fiery in spirit and fought strong in her rebellion, but he'd broken her down over time, beating her into submission.

In all, she had come to know his true preference of rape over mutual consent. With that, she understood he was in dire need of psychiatric counseling and he was indeed guilty of the charges she had defended him against.

Ashley believed in God– as her fiancé had taught her– and had followed his word as faithfully as the human heart would allow. She was well aware of the misstep with her infidelity, and she felt her current situation was God's retribution. She had lost temporary sight of God in being with James, for he was a nonbeliever and wanted no such practice under his roof, claiming that God truly didn't exist, that he was merely an enigma for the needy and helpless, of which he was neither. She had hoped to someday have him see otherwise, but the mere mentioning of God brought about an undesirable change in his temperament. With him, she could never broach the subject.

After the turning point in their relationship and being confined to a designated room, she had asked for a Bible, and he had beaten her for it, reminding her that he wanted no such garbage under his roof, that those who believed in such were delusional. The following morning, much to her surprise, he had come to her bearing a leather-bound copy of The King James Version along with a monthly devotional, Our Daily Bread.

"I told you God doesn't exist," he spat and flung them both to the floor. "But now you'll see for yourself. See if your God delivers you from me– because that's exactly what you will pray for! See if he smites the evil one and whisk you away!" He was shouting, furious for reasons she could not understand.

He pointed a trembling finger at the Bible and devotional at his feet. "I told you that shit is garbage for the needy and hopeless, that which you have become, but it will get you nowhere! Do you hear me? Nowhere!" With that, he stormed out of the room and locked the door.

He had been correct in his assessment of her prayers. Upon his exit, she had gone immediately for the Bible and into prayer on the floor, asking God to cleanse away her sins and deliver her from what such has brought. She prayed daily, and James returned just as frequently to remind her that such was useless. Although she did not admit to him, his words began to ring true. In so, she prayed less and hardly studied the Bible, concluding God's reality to be a hoax.

"Did you hear me, girl," James' commanding voice brought her back to the present. "I said turn over and let me have you from behind."

Ashley assumed the position, despondently awaiting his entry. Here it would be worse.

Chapter 2

Trayon Haymon awoke covered in sweat and shivering, his breath like a long-submerged swimmer breaking the surface, his pulse beating a pace to match. He sat up, shook his head to clear what remained of the dream, to no avail. The supernatural and psychic phenomenon was something that went beyond his belief. Thus, there was no logical explanation for his dreams— no, visions. Visions of his fiancée, Ashley, in another man's bed.

A practicing attorney, Ashley had left Savannah for North Carolina six months ago, claiming to have been retained once again in the state. A week after her departure came the unprecedented vision of her sleeping with another. In all his thirty-two years in life, no dream came close to the vivid clarity provided by this one. To his sense of sight, sound, and smell, it couldn't have been more acute if he'd been thrust in the room with them.

Amidst their cries of passion, the bong of a Grandfather Clock, somewhere down the hall, marked off the hour. Trayon awoke to find his bedside clock matching the hour, certain he'd been afforded a glimpse of reality. He'd snatched up the receiver to dial Ashley's cell number but slammed the handset back into the cradle on second thought.

With her call the following morning, her voice held such loving sincerity that he couldn't present her with questions of infidelity, conscious of insulting her with the accusation. Besides, she had never broken his trust. With that, he denied the vision, passing it off as figments of his imagination, his subconscious mind at play.

He dreamt again that night, and there was no denying the truth. When Ashley next called, Trayon said nothing. Night after torturous night he suffered, witnessing her in the arms of another. He kept silent, willing her to come clean with it all and ask for forgiveness, but she did nothing of the sort. She hadn't the least of guilt. The pressure was overbearing, and he eventually came to her with questions.

Ashley protested her innocence, however, but Trayon was certain of the visions' accuracy and nothing she said convinced him otherwise. Adamant in her denial, the conversation ended with anger and pain at her infidelity. He prayed to God, but the visions continued, his distress unabated.

He hopped onto his Suzuki, at times, speeding recklessly through the city and passing police cruisers at break-neck speed, daring them to try and stop him. None did, obviously understanding the futility of such an attempt. Even at speeds exceeding one-hundred miles an hour, Ashley's betrayal couldn't be left behind. He fell again to the use of marijuana, a drug he'd given up years before in finding his way to God. The drug was inadequate; he sought oblivion and peace, but neither could be found, not even in sleep, that which he avoided but inevitably fell to.

In the absence of visions, there were nightmares to take their place and they were equally unsettling. In one nightmare, Trayon had been taking Ashley from behind. He closed his eyes near climax, losing himself in her warm wetness. When next his eyes opened, there was James kneeling before Ashley, a hand to her head as she gave him oral.

"She's good isn't she?" James said, a knowing smile creasing his lips.

Trayon froze in mid-stroke, his face a twisted shock of anger.

"What's wrong?" James taunted. "You don't like to share?"

Trayon awoke panting, reaching for marijuana.

In another, Ashley was getting dressed in their bedroom with Trayon outside the closed door encouraging her to hurry.

"I'm coming," Ashley called.

The door was suddenly transparent, and Ashley wasn't alone. She was with James. He had her pinned to the bed, driving repeatedly into her womanly passage. Her nails dug into his flesh and her expression was ecstatic; she was literally coming.

Trayon was at first immobile. Then he reached for the doorknob in a fit of rage, only to find it absent. Further angered by this, he threw his shoulder at the door. It didn't budge. He kicked and called her name. Either she didn't hear or didn't care, for they kept their rhythmic motion. Trayon pounded and kicked more furiously. Ashley didn't glance in his direction; he was obviously being ignored.

Trayon was frantic: kicking, pounding, and ramming with everything he had until exhaustion brought him to his knees. With that, he could only watch as the two continued their lascivious activity. Sleep was simply undesirable in the face of visions and nightmares such as these.

The manuscript on which he worked, the sequel to the first in a fantasy trilogy, was fast approaching its due date. Such a breach of contract would prove detrimental to his career, yet he could not clear his mind to write. He sat silently before his computer, knowing only thoughts of betrayal and the reoccurring question of why. For years he'd provided for Ashley, and had met the financial requirements for her to attend college. She had said yes to his question of marriage. Her treachery was unwarranted.

In the months to come, the visions portrayed a drastic change in Ashley's relationship with James. No longer was there tenderness between them. James began abusing Ashley and forcing himself on her, using leather belts to make her comply with his demands, going as far as sticking heated silverware to her flesh. At this, Trayon's anger at Ashley was magnified and redirected at James.

Trayon had never stood for anyone so much as raising their voice at Ashley, and he was furious at witnessing the man treat her with such disregard. His first impulse was to fly straight to North Carolina and teach the psycho-nut a lesson. He was balked by the fact Ashley had chosen another and now had to deal with what problems derived from that decision.

Finding James would have presented no true obstacle; the visions revealed his precise location. It also revealed Ashley's confinement and her vain attempts at escape in James' absence. Ashley's prison was secure, impossible to escape without outside aid– aid in which Trayon was more than capable of providing.

Many nights after awaking from visions or nightmares, he had been tempted to lend the hand she so desperately needed, but her betrayal scarred him deep, and he wasn't inclined to forgive. With that, the notion of rescue was only briefly entertained before being discarded.

Now, six months after Ashley's departure, his sleep was continuously disturbed by visions. Having stilled his breathing, Trayon nestled his feet to the carpet, reaching for the lamp on the nightstand. Light flared bright at his touch, pushing shadows to the corners of the room. Would he ever know peace? Would the visions plague him for the rest of his life? And why could he not distance nor detach himself from what they revealed? The sensations wrought were as intense as they had been in the beginning, the continuous effect unnatural.

A half-smoked marijuana blunt sat in the ashtray atop the stand, obscuring the face of a digital clock. It was 2:19. Trayon took the blunt and the lighter, then set flame to the former with the latter.

"I can't take much more of this," Trayon spoke, exhaling a cloud of smoke. But what could he do? His only option was to rescue her and that was out of the question. She would suffer just as he did now. Besides, rescuing her would only eliminate the visions, leaving him with nightmares as a constant reminder. He wanted to speak with someone, to share his pain with another, but who would believe the telling of such extraordinary events? Any listener would summarize that he had construed fiction with reality. He wouldn't be taken seriously; humiliation would be added to his current state.

Having smoked the half down to a stub, Trayon discarded the remains in the ashtray. He suited up for the current conditions, snatched up his keys, grabbed his helmet, and left the house.

An Audi S7 sat in front of the garage, its silver paint and dark tinted windows beaded and streaked with condensation from the night's atmosphere. The motorcycle sat behind the Audi, resting on its double stands. *Shadow*, read the license plate; precisely what it appeared at night with him streaking through the city like a bat out hell. He straddled the bike and started the motor, letting it idle while he strapped on the helmet.

A glance back at the house brought a whimsical shake of his head. An exterior construction of red-brick with multiple rooms and a screened side porch overlooking an in-ground pool, the house no longer held for him the comforting sense of home.

Abandoned by his father, raised by his mother alone, Trayon had known poverty throughout childhood. His mother provided books in place of toys, from which came his affinity for reading as well as his exceptional grasp of the written language. He was well into creating worlds of fiction in lavish contrast to his own world by his freshman year in high school.

Trayon's talent caught Phillis Powell's attention, the music instructor and play director at Savannah High. He wrote plays for Ms. Powell, and in his junior year she helped him to publish his first novella, bringing about his status as a flourishing author by graduation. He met Ashley and was happy, her presence which gave his house the definition of home.

"Son," his mother had cautioned some years ago. "Success at a tender age is rare. Rare still are first love relationships that last a lifetime. God has blessed you, and you've come to live without a care in the world."

"What exactly do you mean?" he'd questioned, baffled by the parable.

"Life on earth can never be perfect," she said. "Although the sky is bright, there will be days of cloud and rain. It should never catch you unprepared."

Her words were puzzling, and he'd gone from his mother's home with no real understanding. Only after Ashley's treachery, the conversation all but forgotten, did he comprehend his mother's caution. With more experience in life than he, she was well aware an individual's attention could stray and neither deeds nor love was enough to keep one faithful. Such was his love for Ashley, his mother had known he'd hear nothing of her attempt at addressing the matter directly.

Life on earth can never be perfect, his mother's words came to mind as he guided the motorcycle out of the driveway, throttling gently with consideration to the neighbors and the residential speed limit of 25 miles per hour until he came to White Bluff Road. Here, the speed limit was 45 miles per hour. As always with this kind of ride, he gave no regards to the speed limit, throttle wide open, the motor bellowing loud in the early morning night.

North, his current direction of travel, was more to the inner city where traffic lights were frequent and excessive speed more hazardous. With green lights for blocks to come, Trayon twisted the throttle further, spurring the motorcycle to greater speeds.

At the intersection ahead, a car approached from the east, stopped briefly and made a northbound turn, miscalculating Trayon's distance and speed, pulling out in front of him. Trayon's response was immediate, leaning hard to the left with the simultaneous squeeze on the hand brake. It was a terrible mistake, he knew the moment he'd executed the maneuver. His front tire struck the curb, the rear followed, and the bike was suddenly airborne– caught abruptly by an oak tree along the median…

Chapter 3

Trayon opened his eyes to darkness, waiting for them
to adjust. Complete, the darkness remained. He
brought a hand to within inches of where he gauged
his face to be. He saw nothing. Strange. His mind
went racing. Why couldn't he see? Had he somehow
gone blind? He noted his position, that he was neither
lying, sitting, nor standing, but... suspended... in
darkness. He questioned the assessment, stretching
out and about; his limbs came in contact with nothing.
Something was wrong. Very wrong. He delved
within, assessing the situation, and for a second there
was nothing.

Then it came; the unlawful trek down White Bluff,
the car turning in front of him and his deft maneuver
to avoid it. He recalled striking the curb and

becoming airborne… and now. But what and where is now? To speculate was dreadful. Am I really dead? If so, where are the others? Better yet, where's the tunnel of light many claim to see when brushed by death?

"*Unfortunately*," a voice penetrated the darkness. "*You'll never see the tunnel, the light, nor the world beyond it for that matter.*"

Trayon twisted, seeking the entity from which the voice had come. There was darkness only, but he knew, such was the power it carried, the voice belonged to God. With what had been implied, caterpillars spun cocoons and became butterflies in his stomach. He considered the possibility of God teasing. But would he play such a game? With that came fear, the likes of which he'd never known in life. It spoke of doom beyond that of mortal means.

"How can that be so?" Trayon said into the darkness, his voice strange to his own ears. "I gave my life to you and followed your word as best I could."

"*That is so*," God spoke. "*But you failed the final test.*"

Again, Trayon sought the source of the voice. It seemed to emanate from the very air itself. "What test is that?"

"*Forgiveness*," God spoke.

Trayon was lost.

"You see," God went on. ***"When Ashley commenced to being unfaithful, I sent visions and allowed you to bear witness to the proceedings. Later, when things went sour, you saw this as well. I gave you her location, yet you did not rescue her. So hurt were you by her act of betrayal, you were conscious of your decision to leave her in the hands of someone you called a madman. That is an act of revenge.***

"Trayon, my son, you know well; take not an eye for an eye, but turn the other cheek. Your decision with Ashley is incorrect by me."

The darkness split before him, visually reminiscent of parting drapes bringing forth light. Below, miles perhaps, a sea of red spanned as far as the eye could see. Heavy waves rolled the surface, surging as if provoked by violent winds. A reflection of the color of the water below, the sky remained relatively clear, however; not a single cloud, nor did there appear to be a breeze.

A survey of the sky revealed neither sun, moon, nor any source from which came the light. He looked again to the rolling sea— and flinched at the new horror that greeted him, though there was nothing "new" about it. The sea was indeed the source of light. What he'd initially taken as waves were nothing other than enormous tendrils of flame.

Trayon's earlier fear gave way to terror. He had no misconception about the fire; it was for him. From below came the wailing of billions of souls, screaming, pleading for mercy; unlike any he'd heard in life. It never occurred to him the human voice could portray such agony, and his mind reeled with the knowledge that his own cries would soon echo that of those rising from the flames.

"Oh, God," Trayon moaned. "Please forgive me."

"I'm sorry, my son, but your heart is impure, and only in life can you redeem yourself and ask for forgiveness."

The remaining darkness disappeared. No longer was he suspended in space. He was falling, tumbling head over heels toward the hellish inferno, the Lake of Fire, where the flames were seven times hotter than the fires of earth, where his soul would burn for all of eternity.

Chapter 4

Trayon came slowly to consciousness. The soft but steady cadence of an electronic chirp and the smell of antiseptic alerted his waking mind to panic. The memory was prevalent, visiting upon him those horrific moments of the crash. Clear was the bike's rumble between his thighs. Clear was plastic breaking, metal collapsing, and fiberglass crunching–violently.

Trayon shuddered, visualizing the car turning and spurring him to action, that which he'd immediately regretted with his airborne trajectory to one of many oak trees home to the median. Having cursed his instinct in that nanosecond, he knew now they had saved him twice: avoiding the car and the split-second decision to throw himself clear of the bike before it met violently with the tree.

Darkness filled his consciousness, replaced now with a vision of fire, a sensation of falling, a moment's fear– then it was gone. It couldn't be placed, nor did he understand, but the resulting chill was undesirable.

The electronic cadence sounded at shorter intervals, tracking his accelerated pulse. Trayon's eyes snapped open– and the fluorescent rays attacked his pupils, forcing his eyes shut. He welcomed the pain, unjustifiably weary of encountering darkness. He cracked his eyelids, peeking over at the figure he'd glimpsed resting on the recliner-bed, a figure who sat upright now, her attention drawn by the EKG's erratic tones. He recognized the woman, her expression more concerned than expectant. She looked from him to the machine, and back again.

"Momma?" Trayon called, his parched throat reducing his voice to a hoarse whisper, alien to his own ears. She gazed silent and unmoving. He frowned, swallowed and called to her again. She left the recliner and came to his bedside, reaching over the rail and taking his hand.

"Oh, baby," she said. "I didn't think you were awake."

Trayon's brow furrowed. "Didn't you hear me?"

"I heard, but you've called out several times over the weeks and you weren't awake then either. The good Lord has answered my prayers." Her voice soft, her expression that of concern. "What happened, Trayon?"

His response was immediate. "I crashed my bike."

She shook her head. "It's more than that. I've known for a while but kept quiet in figuring you'd work it out. Your visits to me were less frequent and your excuse was work related. Credence is in Ashley's absence with you. She was always off handling a case." She stroked his hand with her thumb. "I've been here every day since your accident, but she has shown up not once, when it's obvious from your semiconscious ranting you wish otherwise. I know your love for the girl. You wouldn't do anything to hurt her, but I somehow feel her absence isn't her fault."

Trayon's neutral expression belied his thoughts. Semiconscious ranting? Wish otherwise? Not her fault? Then whose fault was it? he wanted to ask, choosing instead to remain silent.

"Yes," his mother continued. "You crashed your bike, but more than likely as a result of what's bothering you. Whatever's the problem, Trayon, it's destroying you, and that in turn brings suffering to me.

Somehow you must come to terms with this. You must fix it."

Swinging on near silent hinges, the door opened to emit the body of an elderly nurse. A stethoscope hung from her neck to rest over an ample bosom. She carried a clipboard in hand and a medical instrument in the other.

"I see you're here completely this time," she greeted Trayon. "That's good." She smiled at Trayon's mother. "And how are you today?"

"Joyful," his mother replied.

"That's good. That's good. Just give me a second to get his vitals and I will be out of your way."

"Take your time." His mother slid away from the bed. "I was just leaving. I can go home and rest easy now. That recliner becomes quite uncomfortable."

"I'm sure it does, honey," the nurse agreed.

Trayon suffered his mother's meaningful gaze. "Sunday over dinner," she said and turned away. He shifted uncomfortably and was alerted to the stiffness of body. He would have to spill it all. Which wouldn't have been a problem under normal circumstances, but this was anything but normal. In all the history of Sunday dinners with his mother, he could remember none less anticipated than this.

"If you don't mind me asking," the nurse questioned. "Who is Ashley?"

"Why that particularly?" Trayon countered.

"You ranted unintelligibly but 'Ashley' was most coherent and repetitive. You would come through for a second then slip away. With only minor head injury, Dr. Kilby suggested your coma was self-induced, psychological trauma as opposed to physical. He implied that you were subconsciously withdrawing as refuge."

Trayon nodded. "She was my fiancée."

"Was?" the nurse inquired, holding a thermometer before his face.

"Um-hmm," he confirmed, accepting the thermometer under his tongue. And how was he to explain that to his mother?

Chapter 5

Two days later, after his caretakers were certain he wouldn't slip away and his bladder functioned without a catheter, Trayon was released from the hospital. His home of four bedrooms, upon entering, always warm and welcoming, was silent, lonely, and cold; as it had been for months now. It wasn't so homey with Ashley's absence. Off handling a case, the house never felt so dead, for he knew she'd return, ever loving and faithful.

Trayon strode through the front room and willed himself not to look in the kitchen as he went. He managed, but to what avail? He could avert his gaze but he could not help visualizing Ashley's smiling face looking up from the stove in warm welcome. In the past she would pause long enough to kiss him, announce what was cooking and how long before it was served.

Ashley was thoughtfully attentive, and Trayon appreciated the gesture, never neglecting to demonstrate his appreciation; which made her perfidious conduct all the more elusive, unwarranted. Such behavior seemed more befitting to a callous individual, and Ashley was anything but callous. He knew this in his heart but the visions contradicted that certainty.

A pile of letters at the bed's center awaited him in the bedroom. His mother had been keeping what little in perspective in his absence, he realized. Something he should have known at finding only a few letters in the mailbox, those of which having fairly recent postmarks. The fact he hadn't made the observation clearly indicated his perception wasn't up to par. He plopped down with it all, preferring Ashley's company over accumulated mail. He couldn't deny the fact he missed her, but the wounds of treachery has yet to heal and he wouldn't accept her back if permitted. Though he didn't care particularly for the situation that bound her, he felt underlying satisfaction at her misfortune, begotten by treachery.

Trayon suffered a wave of déjà vu: a flash of darkness, a vision of fire, a sensation of falling, a moment's fear– then it was gone. The flash seemed a true memory, yet he couldn't place it as one. An experience that spawned so dramatic a response, he mused, wouldn't be so easily misplaced nor forgotten. However, he wasn't pressed to know its origin considering the sensation associated with such. He, instead, turned his attention to the phone atop the nightstand. A pulsing green dot on the machine blinked rhythmically, its console signifying numerous missed calls and voice messages.

He sighed, reaching out to activate The Message Center on speakerphone. There were twenty messages, eight marked urgent.

Urgent message, came the digital voice. *Marked Tuesday fifteenth, nine fifty-four a.m....*

"Trayon?" a male's voice followed.

Trayon winced, mentally bracing at hearing his agent.

"Newberry, here," the voice continued. "You've been absent for three consecutive signings. Thought I'd check in with you about that. Give me a call if there's a problem with the itinerary."

The message ended and there was another, dated some three days after, in regards to Trayon's continued absence in subsequent events. Newberry questioned whether Trayon had gotten the e-mail containing the scheduled appearance, asking him to call upon receipt of the message. Every message left by the agent was more heated than the one before until the man was yelling, practically spitting every word into the phone.

"I don't know what in the hell is going on with you, Trayon." Newberry's angry voice snarled from the speaker. "Skipping out on appearances isn't good for business. Even so, I wasn't tripping the matter. But now *Mystics of Roth*'s sequel is due on my desk in three days, Trayon, and I haven't heard anything from you in months. At *Sun Star* we play by strict rules son, and you're in breach of contract! My word contributes a lot to my line of work, and I've made my mark on deliverance, on solidity! I've built my career with dependable authors. I told you to stick with fiction; fantasy isn't your field!

"I went out on a limb for you with this. You promised a trilogy and that's exactly what I need. You're pushing it, buddy! *Gemstone* is spitting fire at the agency! You're above novice. You should've foreseen trouble far enough in advance to warn me. Don't scar me on this, Trayon. I want that manuscript!"

The threatening reprimand, for it could be nothing else, brought to a head Trayon's true peril. He recently traversed a course which, if continued, would surely see his career to an end– a fact which hadn't bothered him before. That in itself was absurd considering the fact his wealth and continued livelihood depended upon his ability to produce fiction. Though well off, he wasn't yet set to fall back. He reprimanded himself mentally for sinking so low and disregarding consequences of detrimental effect. Though his love for Ashley is profound, he scolded himself for allowing her to drive him near destruction.

In fiction, characters often fell victim to such. He himself has given birth to stories of a similar nature and knew several cases in real life where people were outright driven to suicide. Love was powerful. Even so, it was his belief that one could endure the trials of betrayal, that one could know hurt and not self-destruct or wither away and die as a result. Those who succumbed were weak, a weakness he despised in men. He knew contempt for self and was forced to acknowledge his accident for the near suicide it was.

No human, he mused, should ever allow another to wield such power over oneself. Trayon was determined to shrug off the cloud of darkness and reclaim the light of happiness.

Whatever the problem, Trayon, his mother's words came to mind. *It's destroying you, and that in turn brings suffering to me. Somehow you must come to terms with this. You must fix it.* His mother's words lent strength to his resolve as he picked up the phone to return his agent's call.

"Sun Star Agency," a male answered on the third ring. "Newberry speaking."

Trayon took a deep breath before identifying himself. There was a beat of silence and then came Newberry's harsh line of furry, and Trayon, feeling the other's wrath as justified, endured the tirade in silence, which ran strong for the duration of minutes before the man began repeating himself, and finally demanded a "damn good explanation."

Only then did Trayon, with sketchy details, relay his dilemma, ending with the comatosely crash of his motorcycle. At which Newberry softened, expressing something of compassion with questions regarding his mental capacity.

"No brain damage if that's what you're getting at," Trayon supplied. "I've yet to write, as I'm merely hours out of the hospital, but I'm capable."

"In that case, Trayon, get to work. I need that manuscript."

"Sure you do."

"So," Newberry pushed. "Finished and on my desk in a week?"

It was neither question nor request.

"Finished and on your desk in a week," he conceded.

"Good." Newberry rejoiced. "And you can shoot right on up to Virginia immediately after. You'll be speaking at K.D. Hampton Library in Richmond, flying to California thereafter and meeting with Milligan."

Trayon felt bombarded but didn't let on. "K.D. Hampton? That's new territory. What's their request?"

"No request. The library is addressing AIDS awareness and wanted an author who'd recently put out catching material on the subject. They were sifting through the channels, and I booked you!" Newberry chuckled. "We go that extra mile for you here, Trayon. I have to admit you have a unique approach to the subject, but Milligan reached personally."

Trayon was taken. *Sun Star* did go that extra mile. It wasn't a stretch to comprehend Newberry's anger; when the agency produced, he was expected to uphold his end. "You mean Lady Milligan?"

"You bet," Newberry said. "A three hour workshop at her store in Redondo Beach."

"She doesn't even know me."

"In this business, by name and reputation, millions will know you."

"I'm aware," Trayon was tolerant. "What's her pitch?"

"It's on self-publishing," Newberry stated. "She wants you to lead."

"I see." Trayon said. Having made quite an impression in the field, no further explanation was necessary.

"So," Newberry prodded. "Are you up to it?"

Another question with only one answer. "Certainly," Trayon said.

"Good. I'll get back to you shortly with more details. Godspeed on that manuscript."

"Um, Newberry?" Trayon called to the man.

"Yeah, what's that?"

"Just so you know; Fantasy *is* my field."

"Sure it is, buddy."

Chapter 6

The smallest of four bedrooms, the study was situated to accommodate the writer, furnished with refrigerator, microwave, couch, and shelves of books. A Dell PC topped a dark Edgewater desk, behind which sat a navy blue Tempur-Pedic chair, positioned at the room's center to offer the seated individual a panoramic view through the picture-window overlooking the backyard and the wooded area beyond.

Retrieving a sprite from the fridge, taking a seat behind the desk and switching on the Dell, Trayon accessed the latest file of *The Mystics of Roth*, familiarizing himself with the document. He rolled his shoulders– winced at the stiffness –and set out to complete the final chapters.

The flow was great, one sentence after another. He found himself grinning, experiencing his usual excitement at the plot's unfolding, unable to recount when last it flowed so rich; paragraph after paragraph. He dug in with the single-minded focus that was his natural approach to writing, time sliding away as his fingers danced over the keys. Several thousand words concluded the chapter and suddenly he couldn't write; the flow had come to a halt.

With his free-flowing thoughts, the way in which words had seemingly sprung from his mind and onto the screen, he'd anticipated no trouble with subsequent chapters. He thought to breeze through for hours, as is his way upon finding the niche. The problem, he understood, was with the chapter's viewpoint character. He'd created a fiery woman in the likeness of everything that was Ashley, different only in name. Of this Ashley was unaware, for his intent had been to present her with it upon completion. A token of love and flattery, it would certainly portray how intimately attuned his mind is to hers, to the way she thought and felt, his view of her as a near-flawless creature.

He'd been excruciatingly careful in this, scrutinizing every thought and reaction given to the character, ensuring an accurate portrayal. The task required his focus with Ashley, which had, before her betrayal, filled him with elation, an echoing sense of what his feelings were for her.

Now, what with the ramification, to say such focus was disturbing would be the least, for all that would surface were visions of betrayal. How was he to convincingly characterize a character when the model itself brought to mind sensations and moods that fell in contrast to everything he aimed to create?

Exasperated, Trayon leaned back in the chair and stretched, gazing absently around the room. His eyes came to rest on the enlarged, framed photos of Ashley. He'd shot them himself, having taken her by surprise in all three, and the day of their taking was ever clear in mind. They were on Tybee's pier. Her back was to him as he'd just returned from the car with the camera. The sun was minutes above the horizon, a golden disk rising out of the Atlantic.

"Ashley?" he'd called impulsively, camera ready. She turned, her questioning gaze bright with innocence. Her dress was wind whipped and so were strands of her yarn-braided hair, which added to her appeal as she was caught tugging the strands away. He snapped her picture.

"Trayon!" she screamed at him, fist clenched near her breast and smiling. The wind whipped her hair about her neck and shoulders. "Don't do that!" He snapped a second picture, catching her wide spread smile. "Oh, my God!" she screamed, her hands coming to her face with girlish embarrassment. At that moment she was more beautiful than the sun rising at her back. He snapped a third picture.

"God damn you, Ashley," Trayon said aloud now, snatching his eyes away from the wall pictures and closing his mind to the memory. "What in the hell were you thinking?" He pushed angrily away from the desk and paced the room, coming to stop at the picture window overlooking his backyard and the wooded area beyond.

He sought a vision of peace, a glimpse at the animal life therein; the foraging squirrel, a rabbit, a prowling fox. Nature brought him tranquility. Of all, he enjoyed catching sight of the deer. There was something to those big dark eyes; ever watchful. The creature portrayed a sense of innocence, a gentle grace that belied its power when angered or frightened; the fierce locking of horns with a rival; tearing through vegetation impervious to man. It wasn't often he caught sight of the deer, but often was his attempt. The visual, when successful, was only a span of seconds. But there were those rare moments like the last.

Months earlier, midways through the current manuscript, he'd come to a fork in the plot. Troubled, indecisive, he stood at the window. The lawn outside sparkled with early morning dew. A light fog rolled out from the trees, and had it been any heavier, the doe and fawn, just on the other side of the fence, would've been blanketed from view. Trayon held his breath, unwilling to move, afraid of startling the creatures away. For long moments he watched them move about, drifting to and from, grazing, appearing sometimes as only outlines in the mist.

The door opened behind him and Ashley entered. "Honey," she had said. "I brought you break–"

Trayon motioned for silence and beckoned her over to him, never taking his eyes off the deer, fearing they'd disappear if he even turned for a second. Ashley came to him bearing a plate of grits, eggs, sausage, and bacon. He gathered her in his arms, her back to his chest, and together they watched mother and fawn move through the trees and fog alike.

He saw nothing now, and the unbidden memories of Ashley stirred sensations of longing which only fueled his anger. Staring out over his property and over that which is not his, Trayon was forced to acknowledge the fact his entire surroundings, in one way or another, is reminiscent of Ashley. By that same token he was reminded of her treachery at every turn. With that, he was more angry, feeling something of gratification at Ashley's misfortune.

Trayon suffered a sudden wave of déjà vu: a flash of darkness, a vision of fire, a sensation of falling, a moment's fear– then it was gone. The impression was brief but total in its duration, blotting out the world and replacing it with a vision vivid enough to contest reality. Though he couldn't fathom its origin, the experience had overtaken him several times since awakening at the hospital. It felt like a definite memory, yet he rejected the notion. Surely one would remember that which bears such intensity, the promise of death. Though strange, the visions pertaining to Ashley were unquestionably accurate. But what of this reoccurring flash? They were connected, somehow, and he was shaken by it; afraid to where he wouldn't consider it further.

He left the window and helplessly paced the room, his distress growing by the second. Somehow he had to complete that manuscript. Time was ticking and he was at a stand-still.

Whatever's the problem, Trayon, his mother's words came to mind…. *Somehow you must come to terms with this. You must fix it.*

It seemed sound advice, advice he longed to follow. But try as he might, pushing Ashley from his thoughts was no easy feat. The reality of it, the fact he sought to push on and couldn't, complicated matters. He had but one option: complete the manuscript in a week or else. He knew his talent as a writer and was more than confident he could meet the deadline. A clear mind was needed. He stopped short of the window and returned quickly to his desk, pulling open the top drawer. There along with a supply of CD's, flash drives, markers, and pens, a box of White Owl blunts was there with a quarter-ounce bag of marijuana.

A hint of a smile fronted his lips as he took a seat and extracted weed and blunts, inhaling the fragrance through the bag. He would have a smoke, cruise out south around the lake, then return home and begin the next chapter. His smile broadened in contemplating the task. Not only would he begin the chapter, he would complete two to three consecutively. He snatched up a blank sheet of paper from the printer feed and used it as a place-mat in first breaking down then dumping tobacco from the blunt. He moistened the leaf, filled it with marijuana and proceeded to roll it tight, examining the finished work appreciatively. He dried the blunt with a lighter from the drawer and was suddenly conscious when last he'd gotten high and gone out for a ride.

Unbidden came the panic stricken moments before a deadly crash that left him comatose for weeks. He sat aside the lighter and blunt, never one to disregard a lesson; for that is precisely what the accident had been. He'd known better, having given up drugs years ago, finding reverence in God. The ramification with Ashley had caused a relapse. In his distress and want for peace, he'd fallen to drugs and reckless behavior, neglecting the one being that could place matters in perspective.

Rising from the desk and covering the short distance, he sank to his knees before the couch. Palms together, fingers steepled and head bowed, he prayed fervently, begging God to forgive his negligence, pleading for deliverance and peace. He held nothing back, pouring his heart out, stressing his need for guidance, his need for light in this hour of darkness. Long moments he prayed, sincere in his requisition of God's grace.

Little by little the distress and anger dissipated until all that remained was acceptance for what had become of Ashley, peace, and tranquility. Prayer complete, Trayon rose– faltered and stumbled forward onto the couch. He thought to catch himself and was surprised again when his arms buckled, sending him face first into the sofa's back. He rebounded onto the seat to where he lay panting, grimacing at the shock of sore tendons newly subjected to stress. His muscle, weight, and strength were diminished, an actuality he was reminded of with the most unostentatious of movement. Again he felt disgust at having been reduced to a mere shadow of his former self.

No woman, he mused, should wield such power! Not over him at least. Trayon pushed gingerly away from the sofa, padded over to the desk and sat before the monitor. Rolling his neck, rotating his shoulders while placing his hands at the keyboard, he stilled himself and began to type. As he'd prayed, the words came; slow at first, but more steady as he delved deep into the character that was Ashley's mirror.

He was distraught with the effort, for the task kept foremost the essence of the woman he sought to replicate. He wasn't to be discouraged however. Having found the flow, he clung to the more pleasant memories, steeling himself against her deceit and treachery. He typed for hours, pausing periodically between paragraphs, scenes, and chapters to exercise, eat, and relieve his bladder.

It was late when his efforts became increasingly erroneous, having to correct mere words at first, then full sentences and paragraphs as time progressed. He acknowledged his fatigue and called it quits. He would otherwise spend precious time rewriting pages. He contemplated a shower but decided a timeless soak would be more soothing, coming out with marginally less ache and stiffness. He forwent the comfort of his king-size bed, reluctant to feel Ashley's absence, and returned to his study to sleep on the couch with a mind to rise early and begin work anew.

Chapter 7

Trayon slept fitfully, and though he didn't wake early, he prayed and didn't go immediately to his computer as decided the previous night. Instead, he went into the kitchen to prepare himself a balanced breakfast. He was moving forward, no longer subjugated by the past. Fiction held firm to exposition but his life would be that of present and future. Even so, his throat tightened as he withdrew cooking utensils from the cabinet and sat the frying pan on the glass top stove. The digital appliance with its self-cleaning system had been one of the many gifts he'd bestowed upon Ashley over the years. She'd been so delighted in discovering its installment in place of their old one.

"Oh," she'd exclaimed, pressing buttons and assessing its functions. "It even has a timer." She turned to face him, all smiles and delight, stepping close. "Is there anything in particular you'd like?"

He circled his arms around her waist and kissed her brow. "I now have what I like, but I'm happy with whatever you prepare."

Her appreciation for the stove was genuine, Trayon mused, now scrambling eggs. She always seemed appreciative and grateful. In retrospect, she'd been anything but. Anger surfaced and he suppressed it, unwilling to be trapped. He must move on. The sooner the better. He'd made the mental decision and must now make it reality. He carried a plate of hash browns, eggs, and sausage into his study, sitting behind the desk and switching on his computer. He ate slowly, reading over the last chapter, letting his mind play at what's to come, mapping the blueprint he would physically replicate.

Trayon's excitement grew as ideas formed and pieces that eluded him the previous night fell into place. He consumed his breakfast with increasing vigor, eager to write, having once again struck the vein of flow. Trayon stuffed what remained of his eggs into his mouth, pushed the plate aside, and wiped his hands on a napkin. Squaring shoulders that bespoke his trauma, he set hands at the keyboard with fingers poised to write. Words flowed and he was soon caught within the world he created, crafting with a single-minded focus that was his way. Time warped and his fingers strove to keep pace with thought; the sort of chase that led to the most gratifying end, that which he sought now.

Several times throughout the hours, however, fingers took over and it was then he took to stretching and exercising his body, allowing his mind to cast out, leaving the trail to follow. The routine carried him through the day and well into the night. When he did retire, it was to his bed where he set his mind firm against the empty space beside him. For two days he repeated the routine, each night less tense and more relaxing as there were no visions or haunting dreams of Ashley. Absent also were those intense flashes of doom. He was positioned on the gray carpeted floor of his study, stretching, when he received his first call.

"Trayon?" said the caller. "Have you forgotten? You should've been here by now."

Though early, he thought it was Newberry and was surprised to hear his mother. Only at her question did he recall the day of the week. Though her tone was questioning, there was no option of refusal. She wanted him over for Sunday dinner. It was his mother as he'd always known her, prompting him to lay bare his troubles. She'd become rather patient as he'd gotten older, pressing only if the problem met no remission. As was the case here.

Trayon exhaled into the receiver. "I guess I did, momma, but not intentionally."

"I bet," she countered.

He laughed, knowing she was at that very moment envisioning his many attempts to avoid encounters similar in nature. "Seriously, momma, I'm way behind and pressed to complete this manuscript. I lost track of time. How about dinner some other day?" He knew it wouldn't fly.

"Behind schedule?" she intoned. "It must be worse than I imagined. This ought to be interesting. How long before you're here? Dinner is ready now."

"Come on, momma. I have Newberry breathing down my neck and issuing threats."

"I'm sure. But considering the circumstances, he certainly must have given you a window. Take a break and start fresh. Besides, you were a bit slim lying in that hospital bed. You should eat and get your weight up."

"I'm eating, momma."

"What? Sandwiches and hot pockets? I'll keep the food warm until you get here. I love you, Tray."

"Love you too, momma." Trayon cradled the receiver, shaking his head and smiling. They were close, the two of them, his love and respect for her, total. Though he preferred otherwise, he would go to her.

She was correct in that he wasn't so pressed as not to attend. It wasn't for him to deny her any reasonable request. Besides, he felt it was past time he spoke with someone. Who better than his mother? There remained only the prospect of visions. They were unexplainable, and his mother would surely think he'd taken too hard of a blow to the head if he were to present her with such.

The day's work was filed accordingly and the computer shut down. He would have to lay down an edited version of events. The problem, however; she would sense the omission and press on it. What then would he say? The monitor went blank and Trayon rose from the desk, his eyes going to the framed photos of Ashley. He stared at each in turn, his gaze lingering on the one caught with girlish embarrassment. "Never did I imagine you'd do this to me," he said, and left the study.

Chapter 8

Trayon sat at the dining table across from his mother. Having told all, he waited with head hung in silence. The meal before him– smothered shrimp with pork chops and gravy-covered rice, collard greens and cornbread– was partially diminished. He speared a shrimp, forked up some rice, and brought the serving to his mouth, casting furtive glances to gauge his mother's reaction. He'd spoken of everything from first vision to accident. There had been no help for it; no variation of events was sufficient. Though accurate or altered, either would seem unbelievable, but he'd felt best in recounting the unbelievable truth.

His mother had been quiet throughout, listening, meticulously reducing her food at a slower rate than he. Her face betrayed a range of emotion and he longed to know why with each. Especially that which surfaced near the end; wonder/recognition/fear– consciously concealed. Several times he thought to pause with a question but stopped himself. There would be time enough after his recount.

"And you dreamed this?" his mother asked now, her first words since the narration began. "Visions, you say?"

"Yes, momma, and I know this all comes off as fiction– who would know better than me –but the visions are as I've mentioned."

"I didn't say otherwise." Her dark eyes held his, her expression calm. "Though I'd like to attribute this fable to your accident, you professed it to have occurred beforehand, the accident a direct or indirect result."

He was hopeful. "Then you believe me?"

"I believe you are convinced it is as you have told."

Trayon was taken aback. "Come on, momma. I'm delusional?"

"It would seem so, but what other explanation is there?"

"I don't know, but it is what it is."

"Okay." She set down her fork and plucked the pork chop between forefingers and thumb. "Let's say it is. Are you still plagued by them?"

"Not since the accident."

"And you intend to do what now?"

"What else?" he said. "I'll move on as I would have done had I not been imprisoned by these visions.

With them, I couldn't mend as I can now. Everything I felt– love, admiration, hurt, betrayal, the sense she was mine and I longed for her to remain so –was prevalent, unnaturally so." He shook his head. "No longer."

"And what of Ashley?" his mother asked.

"What of her?" he countered. "She pays the price for her choice."

Her eyes flashed angrily and her brows knitted. "So do you for being so foolish!"

Trayon recoiled. "Foolish?"

"Yes! Foolish, hateful, and stubborn to the point you destroy yourself in being so! You loved her as none before, yet observed her trapped and did nothing? 'Distressful', you said it was to watch? It would seem logical– no, apparent that nullifying the threat would in turn banish the visions. But you didn't do that, did you? No! And why not? Because you accepted it in order to have her pay, knowing her suffering to be greater. You refused to help her, for if so, she'd be free of torture, leaving you with perceived betrayal."

Perceived betrayal? Trayon wanted to question but dare not interrupt. She was angry, her voice having risen noticeably, and he couldn't remember when last she'd spoken so to him. "It would be unfair, right?" she continued. "That she'd suffer no more while you held the memory of her failings? Did it ever occur to you that she'd remember her own mistake? Of how and what it had cost her? The experience would be with her forever, Trayon. Would it make you feel better to know she suffers far greater than you? Huh, Trayon? Well, she does!"

"Momma, please!" he said finally, increasingly uncomfortable under her misplaced rebuke. "You're acting as if I did this to her. I didn't make her cheat. It is something I never wanted."

"But because she did and was trapped, you refuse to help her?" she pressed.

His response was long in coming. "And for that I'm wrong?"

She struggled with indecision, and he expected from her another parable. "It is for you to decide," she said, "for you must carry the burden."

"I'm certain what befalls Ashley is of no further concern of mine."

She stared at him for long seconds. There was something of fear in her eyes, concealed, then concern took its place. "I didn't raise you this way," she said.

"You cautioned me to mind my own business."

"And are you so sure this isn't your business?"

"Quite sure," he spoke adamantly.

"Have you ever asked yourself why she did it?"

"A million times, and there is no legitimate answer."

"Ask again and look deep. Are you praying?"

"Yes."

"Then pray for guidance, son, it's what you need right now." She bit off a piece of cornbread. "So, how far behind are you?"

Trayon breathed deep and exhaled, comfortable with the new subject. He explained how the current manuscript had been due before the accident and his distraction with the incidents surrounding Ashley. He recounted the heated messages left by his agent, his upcoming conference at the library in Richmond, and the California trip to follow.

"Wait a minute," his mother interrupted, her fork poised midways to her mouth. "How is it you qualify to speak on AIDS and you have no published material on the subject?"

"You remember *Pleazotic*? I submitted it a little after book one of *Roth*"

"Oh," she said, the fork resuming its journey. She chewed slowly and swallowed. "I thought you said that thing would wait until after the trilogy?"

"That thing," Trayon knew, was a sure indication of her disregard for the book. The graphic subject matter was a bit strong for her liking. It remained his only work she hadn't read, and hadn't been in the least eager for him to complete. Her brow furrowed and he knew she contemplated the book's summary.

"The ending was clear," Trayon said. "I felt it necessary to finish, although Newberry advised otherwise, fearing interference with the trilogy production. He wanted no threat to the contract, but I know my talent as a writer and went on to knock ot out. He even questioned whether it had anything to do with the current delay."

"Does it?" she asked.

"Of course not. It was everything that happened with Ashley."

"Son, you should never allow an individual to have that kind of power over you. It threatens everything you have built, all that you have become."

His sentiment exactly. "I know, momma."

"So," she said, an anticipatory twinkle in her eyes. "What's new in the second book of *Roth*?"

"Quite a bit." He kept a straight face. "Unfortunately, you're going to have to wait like everyone else this time."

"What?" She was incredulous. "Are you serious?"

"Most definitely."

She scolded him from across the table. He maintained a blank expression and it was all he could do to keep from smiling. "Boy, watch I bus' you!" she threatened. Such was often a childhood application when he straddled the line. His humor burst forth upon hearing it now.

"You're not funny, you know?" she heartily complained.

Trayon sobered. "I haven't heard that from you in years! I love you, momma."

"I love you, too, Trayon. Now, the second book of Roth, mister."

"Well, the God, Zektor, has agreed to enhance Kendell's medallion."

Her eyes went wide. "Are you serious? With Kendell's potential for evil and his thirst for power, why would the God of peace and prosperity go and do that? And Kendell, a mere practitioner, managed to trick a God into agreeing to such?"

Trayon smiled. "What makes you so sure he was tricked?"

She paused. "I'm not, but I can see no reason why Zektor would provide him with a more powerful talisman."

"Wait and see."

"How about a hint?" she tried.

"Sorry, momma, any more will ruin the plot."

"Ok, enough with Kendell. What else can you tell me?"

It wasn't so much as her wanting the story as it was a teasing taste that kept her anticipating the read. And Trayon knew just how to dangle the plot, as he'd learned to do when he'd written plays for Ms. Powell, the music instructor and play director at Savannah High. His mother had come to see everyone as a result. Likewise, she has read every book he's ever written. All, that is, except *Pleazotic*. She was proud of his success, and he was happy to have her so.

He fed her bits and pieces of plot, answering questions while declining those that would give too much away. Thereafter, conversation fell to more personal inquiries before sliding to casual; mother and son bonding as they had been doing for years from the moment his father had run off, leaving her to raise him alone. Time melted as she spoke on the goings with her floral shop, the small business he'd purchased for her as a Mother's Day gift, and how Aunt Ernestine had kept things running while his mother spent day and night at his bedside in the hospital.

Throughout his childhood and most of his teenage years, his mother had worked two jobs in making ends meet and taking care of him. Always she worked. Even when his income was margin enough to take care of home. Having established himself firm as a writer of fiction, the memory of his mother's struggle and sacrifice ever present in mind, he wanted a cease to her labor, but she insisted she maintain work.

"What am I supposed to do?" she'd countered once. "Sit around and wilt away? Die of boredom?"

"Relax and have fun, momma; God knows you deserve it." She continued to work, and as his financial status increased, so too did his determination to see an end to her labor. He then purchased the floral shop.

"If you must work," he had told her. "It will be for yourself, in your own business." She has since incorporated delivery to its services, boosting the company's status to– surpassing in some cases –that of other floral shops in the city.

"As always, momma," Trayon said long after their meal was finished and they'd spoken at length. "Dinner was nice but I must get going. Newberry's breathing fire about that manuscript. The flow comes easier than it has for months now, and I want this done and wrapped up before he throws in that schedule." He gathered the dishes, took them into the kitchen, and deposited them in the sink, mixing soapy water for them to soak. His mother was there at the table at his return. Her features were troubled, a far-off cast to her eyes.

"What's bothering you, momma?"

She rose, moving to embrace him. "I'm worried about you, Tray." She stepped back to look him over, sliding her hands along his arms.

"Don't be, momma. It hurts but the worse is behind me. Her treachery is but a fading memory. I will move forward from here." She fell in step beside him as he made for the front door, out onto the porch.

The night's temperature was a bit cool for the current season. Dark clouds blanketed the sky, obscuring the stars from view; the fullness of the moon reduced to a faint impression behind the overcast, giving the illusion of a colder night.

"No," his mother said. "I mean this whole thing…. Something's not right, and it's scaring me."

"I know, momma. I felt that way, too, in the beginning, but the hold is no more. It's over now."

"Somehow I feel it's far from over,"

Far from over? Her words struck a chord of fear. They were everything he didn't want to hear, and the women's history of premonition made it all the more frightening.

"Be careful Trayon," she continued. "Pray for guidance and call me before you leave.

"I will." He kissed her cheek. "Goodnight, momma."

Chapter 9

Alone on the porch, in the darkness of night,

Trayon's mother stood with arms folded across her
bosom long after her son's Audi had disappeared
from sight. Fresh tears stung her eyes as she cried in
silence. From all she'd gathered, Trayon's time on
earth was limited. She would lose him soon. A child
of God, she could accept that which was the Lord's
will, even when such was as disheartening as the
death of her son, her only child. She did question,
however, him being spared one death only to fall to
another.

"Momma, please!" was Trayon's earlier response to
her verbal reprimand. "You're acting as if I did this to

her. I didn't make her cheat. It is something I never wanted."

"But because she did and was trapped," she pressed. "You refused to help her?"

"And for that I'm wrong?"

In the eyes of the Lord, maybe, she had wanted to tell him, *and that is what truly matters*. Instead, she had said it was for him to be certain, for the burden would be his to carry. Ashley's mishap was of no concern to him, he insisted, but she knew better; his visions were from the Lord. Of this she was certain, but it wasn't her place to tell him; he must come to understand and decide.

God required something of him and she couldn't say what exactly, but Trayon needed to be pure in heart, in thought, and in action. His time was running short, closing to that of a catastrophic end. His soul's salvation was in question. Of this, too, she was certain. It brought to her more misery than the idea of his death; his damnation would separate them for all of eternity. Tears ran fast. Heart heavy, and with a mind to pray, she opened the front door and left the darkness behind.

Chapter 10

Trayon retired shortly after his return home, opting to resume writing after a shower and a long night's sleep, but rest didn't come as easily as it had in the previous nights. He lay in bed tossing, plagued by the visit with his mother. She had been distraught at his recount. Although the proceedings were strange, his mother believed him. More so, he got the impression she knew something of the supernatural aspect regarding his ordeal. There had been a flicker of recognition and fear in her eyes.

At one point she'd become angry, calling him a fool among other things. She struggled with indecision, but said only that he should pray for guidance. He wasn't as religious as she, but he believed in God and was honest in his attempt to follow his word. There was consolation in prayer, and in his wants for such, now, he tossed aside the bed covers, knelt at his bedside and prayed.

He dreamt of Ashley that night, the heightened awareness like that with dreams prior. The first since his return from the hospital, he made no attempt to escape, though history suggested it would be anything but pleasant.

Ashley and Trayon loped through a snow-covered mountain forest. Her coat was white in color, speckled with silver, and in the rays of noon she seemed to shimmer as she darted between winter pine trees with limbs leaden with snow. Her bushy tail, curled high for the most part, swung left to right in counter balancing her weight as she sped through the mountain range. Like her mirror character's portrayal in *Mystics of Roth*, Ashley was a sorceress-mage, having shape-shifted them both to their current forms of holding: Wolves. His coat was dark gray and not half as beautiful as the creature who fled before him.

Up ahead, a cliff gave way to open air and sky, the linear space measuring a quarter mile distance to the far ledge over and much, much further to the valley floor below. Ashley dashed through a tangle of brush, dislodging snow. Trayon followed, knowing a wild sense of freedom born to the essence of the animal he replicated.

Closer to the cliff and open sky with every bound, he expected her to veer away at any given second. She glanced at him over her shoulder, blue/white eyes shining bright, tongue lolling, breath steaming from her muzzle. Flashing a wolfish grin before looking ahead, she stretched further, covering greater distance with every bound. Ashley gained the cliff's summit and leapt out into the open sky. Trayon followed with no regard to his own demise, trusting her to keep them safe.

They fell free for long moments before he was engulfed by Ashley's power, transformed a second time. Below him, Ashley's K-9 form shimmered and underwent a transformation as well. She tripled in size, sprouted wings and became a dragon with bright scales in shades of red, green, and purple. She glared in his direction, her supple neck arched over translucent wings folded over her back, her eyes black-slit pools of amber.

Ashley roared, swatted him playfully across the snout with her tail, twisting belly up and down again, spiraling beautifully away. Her wings snapped open and she beat powerfully at the wind, breaking her descent and shooting skyward.

Bathed in sunlight, her versa-color scales sparkled like thousands of polished rubies, emeralds, and tanzanite. Ashley circled overhead, roaring out her challenge. She folded her wings and dove at him, veering away at the last moment.

Trayon snapped at her tail, stretched his serpentine neck, and beat his wings in pursuit, their playground having gone from mountain forest to open sky. Free, he felt. Truly elated, as only one could in being so magnificent a creature. He gave chase for miles; around snow-capped peaks, between narrow fissures, low over mountain tree tops, tireless in their exotic dance of courtship.

The scene changed abruptly. No longer was there forest, mountain valleys, and open sky. No longer were they flying, and neither was Ashley the versicolor dragon of immense beauty. She was as she had been for some time now; a prisoner in a room and subjected to a madman's whelm. Gone was that haloed aspect inherent in dreams, substituted now by the stark clarity of reality; his dream had become a vision and his majestic sense of euphoria was displaced by apprehension. His attempt to awake was unsuccessful; the vision held fast; he would bear witness to all.

The room door opened and James entered, locking the door behind him, slipping the key into his pocket as he strode to where Ashley lay in bed with covers drawn near to her chin. He gazed, his expression blank. She stared with barely concealed fear.

"Are you naked?" he asked.

Ashley swallowed. "Yes."

"May I see?"

She tossed aside the covers and lay motionless beneath his gaze, hands down at her sides. Her complexion was flawless except for the darkened marks along the right side of her torso where he'd taken heated metal to her flesh in forcing her to comply with his demands. The burns were few, healed over, and would all but fade completely away. She saw the growing bulge at his crotch, and her feet stirred uncomfortably.

"May I touch you, Ashley?" James questioned.

Ashley fumed. "Yes," she said, and James sat beside her, his fingers going first to caress her cheek, trailing down to the hollow of her throat. He kissed her lips and fondled each breast in turn, sliding his hand over her stomach. Here, she intercepted his hand, gently, urging its return to her breast. He halted the gesture, and their eyes met; hers with trepidation, his betraying the undergoing of a struggle within. Seconds ticked away in silence. He sighed deep and returned the hand at her side, lowering his head to lay a light kiss upon her lips.

"Not this night," he told her. "Nor any hereafter. Never again will you have to answer my touch with one of your own." Her eyes flashed something close to gratitude, and for long moments he caressed her stomach, breast, thighs, and hips.

"Turn over," he said. At which her eyes portrayed a school of emotions: suspicion, distrust, disappointment, fear. She hesitated, then obeyed his command, rolling onto her stomach and resting a cheek to the back of her hands, optimizing her view of him.

He touched her shoulder and she flinched at the contact, though the touch was anything but threatening. He ran slow hands down her back and over the generous curve of her tush, down one leg and up the other. Then, ever so slowly, the focus became her butt, James caressing and squeezing with increasing vigor. He concluded with a kiss to either rounded cheek, pulling the covers to her neck and rising from the bed, the bulge at his crotch larger than before.

"Goodnight, Ashley," he said, fishing the key from his pocket. "Put some clothes on, if you like. I won't be back tonight."

He made his exit, the door locked behind him, and Ashley gave slow release to a pinned breath. She rolled onto her side, cradled her head in the crook of her elbow and rocked back and forth.

Trayon woke early that coming morning and for long moments lay contemplating last night's vision and dream. Pleasant, if strange, he regarded the dream a welcome memory considering the toxicity bearing those of late. A beautiful and playful creature is how he saw Ashley. Full of smiles and laughter, it came as no surprise that she'd appeared likewise in his dream as well. He gave thought to himself as the gray wolf plunging over the cliff's edge behind her, trusting her to keep them safe. His life in her hands. Trust. Pure unadulterated trust. So as it had been in reality with him giving her the life of his heart. A means to a catastrophic end; a mistake never to be repeated.

More so now than ever he understood his mother's decision to remain alone after his father's shameless abandonment. "The good Lord is all the man I need right now," she'd said once. It boils down, Trayon summarized, to being safer alone. His mother had been so for years and seemed happy with the fact.

Having been nothing but good to Ashley, her treachery unwarranted, Trayon's current definition of women is synonymous with evil. None would get further than his bed.

The vision itself had been a second reprieve in that it carried neither rape nor violence, though he sensed Ashley's fear and confusion at the man's behavior. She was a raging storm of terror, ever uncertain of James' intent. Trayon also sensed her distaste for the man, the reluctance in granting him permission to exploit her person, to even lay eyes on her body.

Trayon felt rage course through him. Not at Ashley, but at James for his treatment of her. Then, just as quick, he stilled his anger, reminding himself Ashley had made her own bed. He suffered a flash of darkness, a vision of fire, a sensation of falling, a moment's fear– then it was gone.

Trayon bolted upright, released from the clutching grip of fear. He checked himself and slid out of bed with controlled movements. His fingers trembled as he retrieved a robe from the closet. Since the hospital he'd known the dreadful experience, and the sensation brought a notion of doom unlike any known in life. Death, by comparison, didn't seem as horrific.

Both the flash and the visions were associated with Ashley. That he hasn't experienced the last of either, he was certain. The idea of such was sickening, for all he desired is peace and such could not be with visions and horrific flashes of doom.

Chapter 11

Trayon stood before the window in his study, gazing out over the stretch of property that was his and into the wooded area beyond. Having made several false starts at his computer, he now sought the tranquil effect of nature. Just when he thought things were coming together, everything was falling completely apart. The visions were once more upon him. Worse still, his waking hours of sanctuary were threatened with horrific flashes of doom. Though distressful at first, the visions now paled in comparison to the foreboding flash; the implicit promise of his own demise. It crippled his ability to write, which served to stack further against him the opposing forces of time. He had two days to complete the manuscript. Two days before Newberry called upon him to deliver.

He was coming into the height of his career, his name mentioned with the foremost leaders of fantasy. Though reluctant and more than a bit skeptical, Newberry had taken on *Roth* and had since agreed to accept Trayon's sci-fi saga at the completion of *Roth*'s second manuscript. Having begun his career as an author of short fiction with the ultimate goal of mastering genres of sci-fi and fantasy, he was struck hard by the irony of beating back the incapacitating hands of writer's block only to be waylaid by a woman's treachery.

I told you to stick to fiction, Newberry's comment came to mind. *Fantasy isn't your field.*

As far as Trayon was concerned, his talent was boundless and no one could toss hollow statements at him and call them facts. Such was a direct affront. An insult! "I am a genre author of fantasy," Trayon gave voice to his anger, the words coming out a fierce whisper. "Soon to be that of science fiction as well." He returned to his computer, finishing off a sausage and egg breakfast pocket while reading the most recent paragraph, washing down the pocket with a few swallows of sprite. "And I can show you better than I can tell you," he spoke again as he rolled and relaxed his shoulders, setting his finger to the home row.

Letters became words and they in turn became sentences, paragraphs marching up the screen one after another as the flow fell upon him. The world disappeared as he created that of his own, falling to that single-minded focus that was his natural approach in writing. Hours slid by as he repeated the alternating cycle of stretch and exercise, snack and restroom, quiet spells of thought followed by lengthy sessions of typing. The last of which, at one point, was offset by a phone call. Eyes glued to the monitor, right hand dancing over the keys, he reached with the other and placed the call on loudspeaker, left hand resuming its place at the keyboard, fingers typing away.

"Hello?" he answered.

"Trayon?" his mother called.

His fingers went still. "Yes?"

"I'm going to church service with sister Vern and Gloria later tonight. I think you should go with us"

He winced, shoulders eating up his neck, head bowed and turned to one side, face scrunched. "Um, I really need to slide out of this one, momma."

"What you need is God in your life," his mother said.

"I know, momma, but I have to finish this manuscript.''

"Son, it is by the grace of God you even have a manuscript to finish. Trayon come to church with me, please."

Her voice carried desperation, fear perhaps, and he was more certain she kept something from him.

"Momma, I can't. Not tonight. Maybe some other time."

The line was silent. "Many make the mistake of putting off the Lord," she said. "It's never a good thing. There is no later for some."

"I know this all too well, and it's not my intent to push off the Lord, but I'm pressed for time here, momma."

Another bout of silence, a sigh of resignation, then, "Okay Trayon. Maybe next time. I'll have Reverend John say a prayer for you."

"O.K. momma. Love you."

"Love you too, son."

Trayon broke the connection and was unable to type further, so distracted was he by the call. Never in his life had his mother been so adamant in her request for him to attend church. She wasn't one to stress herself with problems in life, not openly at least, but left matters in the hands of the Lord. She would, in regards to him, offer some word of advice or caution. She offered none of either now, and it un-nerved him, for her desperation and fear said everything her words did not; they bespoke imminent danger.

Again he wondered what she knew and why she kept it away if felt so fiercely. Contemplating the matter only served to frustrate him further and made any attempt to write out of the question. Long moments passed before his thoughts were clear enough to resume typing, and longer still until he found the flow and fell in with total focus.

Two days following his mother's desperate request, Trayon completed the manuscript and began immediate preparations for departure. He was scheduled to speak at K.D. Hampton in Richmond, three days hence, and to co-host Milligan's workshop in California, two days after. He slept in the study that early morning-night, too exhausted to make the trip to his bedroom. Here again his sleep was vision filled.

The vision was expositionary in nature, having transpired hours prior to his viewing. As with the visions of the late, he didn't fight to escape, but endured each with a certain level of detachment. James maintained his gentle dealings with Ashley, asking her consent before contact while making neither request nor move at sexual advance, though his desire for such was more than apparent.

Ashley's tension and fear was overwhelming, and Trayon felt her mistrust at James' behavior. She was more than half convinced he'd ravish her at any given moment. Trayon understood the man's nature and also expected him to deliver her a vicious blow.

The blow never came, however, and he should have been relieved. He wasn't; he sensed something amiss, focusing hard on the vision but gaining no insight. James concluded his caressing of Ashley, kissed her and made his exit, locking the door behind him. The vision faded and Trayon slept dreamlessly.

Chapter 12

Clad in a white T-shirt and loose sweatpants, panties and braless beneath, Ashley sat Indian-style atop her bed. She munched absently on a fruit granola bar, deeply engrossed in the unfolding plot of *The Young and The Restless*. Television was one of the few allowances afforded her in her bedroom prison. She suspected the privilege wasn't something attributed to any generosity on James behalf, but an act of cruelty, instead, knowing she'd long for and would be constantly reminded of the world beyond; a world unattainable to her. As a result, she avoided television as much as possible but there was no help for it; the tube was both an available attraction and distraction. That being the case, she found herself viewing more times than not.

Clack! The room door's thrown bolt startled Ashley to panic. The soap-opera and granola bar were forgotten. The latter was tossed aside and that in her mouth, un-chewed, was nearly choked on in her sudden haste to shed her clothing. The T-shirt's threading ripped audibly with the ferocity in which it was pulled over her head, coming clear as the door swung open to announce James' presence.

James drew up short, observing Ashley's frantic attempt with her now knotted drawstrings. "Don't bother," he said, locking the door behind him, moving slowly in her direction.

Ashley's hands went still, falling to her sides. Her eyes were caught by his. His voice carried no anger and his countenance was free of menace, but the fact didn't nullify her fear, however; she hadn't been naked upon his arrival and such had serious repercussions. She glanced at the bedside clock. A redundant gesture in having heard the hall's grandfather clock mark off the hour only moments before. He was early. Way early. And for what reason? To catch her as he had, unprepared, and punish her for it?

The distance between them narrowed to three feet, two... He stopped some inches away, his height of six two towering over that of her five-seven. Her breath quickened. Her heart beat faster, knocking hard at her ribs. She trembled like a rabbit caught in a predator's shadow. She shifted her weight from one foot to the other and back again, uncomfortably under his gaze. She could offer no explanation; it would fall on deaf ears. The fact he'd made an early appearance would count for nothing. He would see, hear, and believe what he wished, that which suited his purpose.

James' hand came up. Ashley flinched inwardly, bracing herself. "May I?" he asked, hand poised near her face.

Strike or caress? She was uncertain as to which.

Though he'd never asked to strike, she wasn't sure now of his intent. After all, she hadn't been naked as is his constant demand, and such didn't go unpunished. What's more alarming is he'd specified nothing in particular; inconsistent with the precise "May I see you?" or "May I touch you?" manner he'd come to favor of late. Was his intent to await her consent and suddenly strike her something vicious?

Ashley withheld her answer, searching his gaze. His eyes slid over her naked torso, returning to hers questioningly. There was hunger therein, a burning lust for the object before him. In times past her body would have responded with a yearning of its own. Now his desire invoked revulsion and terror. Lust didn't alleviate her fear, for she knew firsthand how well his coincided with violence.

Hand poised, he waited. Never had she spoken no to his request. She questioned whether he'd respect it if she did so this time. Staring up into his handsome face of boyish innocence, she ached to refuse him but was weary of the consequences. He would do as he pleased regardless, and if he chose to physically reprimand her slip, her dissension would only serve as fuel to fire.

Ashley breathed deep, bracing further. "Yes," she whispered, and James smiled knowingly, stroking her cheek, sliding his fingers along her jawline to cup the back of her neck, lodging a thumb in her ear to control the tilt of her head. The hold was firm, but not painful. His head lowered as he drew her closer, touching his lips to hers. She breathed a sigh of relief and the gesture parted her lips. He drew her closer, sliding his tongue into her mouth. He caressed her backside as his mouth fell to her neck, down to her breast, sucking at her nipples.

Ashley's slowing pulse quickened. It had been sometime since he'd gone so far with her, having restricted his touch to minimum, his kisses above the neck.

May I? he'd asked, specifying nothing, and like a fool she'd given consent– not that 'no' would have made any difference. Did he want sex? Would he ravish her in the process, or would he simply sate himself and be done with it? She would know soon enough, however, for he now knelt before her, his fingers working at the knotted drawstrings, the tangled mess a result of her haste.

James worked the knot loose with deft fingers, pulling the pants past her hips and down to her ankles prompting her to step out. She complied, contemplating his next move. He planted a quick kiss to her abdomen, caught her up and placed her with care onto the bed. Something grainy pressed at her backside and her physical query turned up the discarded granola bar.

"Here." James held out his hand. "I'll take that if you don't want it." She handed him the half-eaten bar and he commenced eating. *The Young and The Restless*, having gone to commercial, returned to screen, drawing his attention.

"You were watching that?" he asked, more a statement than a question.

"Yes." Her voice was matter of fact, fire bleeding through. "And I would like to see its conclusion, if you don't mind." He cocked a brow. She ran the risk of being struck, but he had intruded and she wanted him aware of her dislike for it.

"It wasn't my intent to disturb you Ashley," he said. "I have something special in mind, but there's enough time for you to watch your stories." He turned and crossed the room, disappearing into her adjoining bathroom.

She heard running water and determined it was the tub's faucet. Something special in mind? What in God's name could it be? There was no telling with him, with all his tricks and treachery. She couldn't remember the last time a "special surprise" or "something for you" turned out to be anything but unpleasant. As had been the case with the double paintings that resulted in him choking her half to death. It was the one incident that terrified her more than any combined. Even now the memory came unbidden.

She had been in bed that night, naked beneath the covers and awaiting his arrival. *Clack*! The deadbolt was thrown and the room door swung in on its hinges. James entered carrying a canvas covered easel which he sat to the floor before retrieving another and placing it beside the first. He locked the door and positioned himself behind either.

"I have a surprise for you," he said.

Ashley sat up, the blanket falling away, neglected in her curiosity. "Really?" she said in spite of herself. Her apprehension dissipated as she knew something of excitement. What fearsome creature this time? She silently wondered, for he was known for capturing the essence of the creature in which he painted: the innocence of a baby chimp, the ferocity of a cougar. The most elusive of animals' characteristics were captured and portrayed in his work. He was renowned for his ability.

Horses were her favorite, and he'd once painted the essence of one in full gallop. It was breathtakingly majestic, a stilled frame of reality it seemed. She could only wonder at what marvel awaited behind the canvas. Was it equine in nature? He knew her preference– and wasn't it a surprise for her?

"Would you like to see now?" he asked, hands on either canvas alike.

"Yes," she said quickly, a smile of anticipation broad on her lips. His art was mesmeric. She couldn't wait. He pulled simultaneously at both canvases, and her widening smile of anticipation froze, went in reverse, and was gone.

The first painting portrayed a woman of light brown complexion garbed in a translucent slip. Caught in the wind, the material billowed about, offering suggestive peeks at her anatomy. She was portrayed from an angle, her gaze head on. Beautiful, sexually radiant, her arms were outstretched, to a lover perhaps, and she wore a smile that none could call anything but genuine. Her features were strikingly familiar, her eyes daunting. They held the utmost terror. She was seriously frightened by something– or someone; conveyed by the eyes alone. The ability was beyond but the most gifted artist, yet he possessed such ingenuity.

The second painting was of the same woman– dressed differently and no less beautiful in her radiance and sexuality –held lovingly by a faceless male. She wore that genuine smile but gazed distantly over the man's shoulder with sad eyes of hurtful longing. That the woman's eyes mirrored her own, Ashley knew instinctively. Tears sprang forth, falling fast down her cheeks. The images alone were disheartening. That they reflected her own dilemma was unbearable. A look in the mirror could not bring to her the sorrow wrought by the paintings.

More distressing was how well James could see it, how he'd captured it so vividly in his art. It spoke clear of his awareness of her trauma, that he fed on it. The crushing blow was the fact he wanted her to know– in ways words could never express. His talent was extraordinary, as she had seen on several occasions, breathtaking, but none before had ever struck such a powerful chord as did these two.

"I see you find them rather touching," James spoke from his stand point behind the easel. He'd watched her in silence, drinking in her reaction. He began undoing his shirt, moving in her direction. "The gallery offered rather generously for the pair, but I declined their offer. These are yours; my gift to you." He tossed his shirt aside and swept his hand in a grand gesture. "Where would you like them hung?" He dropped his pants and boxers, kicking out of both, advancing until he stood just to one side of the bed, his erection mere inches from where she sat. "You know what to do," he said callously.

He wanted her to touch and caress him, for her to take him into her mouth. Tears streaming, she stared, shocked anew at his degree of cruelty. She resented him for it. She resented him, period.

Slowly the covers were pushed aside and she knelt before his erect member. The veins were taut against the skin and it pulsed anticipatingly. She lifted her chin and met his gaze. Her jaw set stubbornly, eyes defiant, "No," she said, holding her position square in front of him.

The boyish innocence contorted into a mask of fury. He swung hard with an open palm aimed at her face.

She fell away from the blow, lashing out and kicking him in the face as momentum brought him forward. She kicked again, but he dodged aside, falling to the bed, rolling to pin her beneath him. She swung with her fists, struck once, then missed as he reared and kept his head out of range.

He returned her attack, driving his fist to her face once, twice– then his hands were at her throat, constricting. She bucked wildly beneath him, clawed at his wrists and forearms, but he wouldn't let go. Black and red dots spotted her vision. Her lungs burned. Her head and face were thick with pressure. Her eyes felt near to bursting out of their sockets. Her pulse pounded hard in her ears.

Black and red bled together and was mostly black, driving her to panic. She fought drastically, digging at his wrist and arms. He squeezed tighter. So tight was his grip, she could neither gag nor gasp. She was slipping away and desperately attempted a new tact, going still under his grip, squeezing questioningly at the hand crushing her throat.

"Please," she mouthed, and with her eyes, she conveyed her defeat, her willingness to submit.

James smiled, and his grip tightened, though she didn't think it possible. He understood and would not accept, would not relinquish his hold. She struck out angrily, her fist making weak contact with his face as darkness swept her under....

Yes, she remembered that night with vivid clarity. She'd regained consciousness with him sexing her. It was the one event which truly made her fear him. The choking drove home the fact he could snuff out her life in a manner far more horrific than beatings. He had enjoyed watching her go, sending her away. It had been in his eyes.

Now, as James re-entered the room, Ashley eyed him intently, wondering at this "something special in mind."

"Relax, Ashley," he said. "You look near to panic. I'm making you a bath. The water is turned so as not to fill as quickly. You can watch your soap-opera as I massage the tension from your shoulders. Now turn onto your stomach."

It was neither question nor request and there was but one acceptable response. She complied. He joined her on the bed and began kneading her shoulders. *The Young and The Restless* plot unfolded with its alternating viewpoints, and by the ending credits her tension had fallen away.

"Is that better?" he asked.

The question was ironic in that his presence is what had first induced her tension. "Yes."

"Now let's have that bath."

The tub was nearly brimming, and the surface rippled in accordance with the dripping faucet, steam wafting visibly about. Ashley drew up short, and James came close to colliding with her from behind. Her heart thundered and she whimpered audibly. Was the water merely hot or scolding? She stepped back involuntarily, colliding with James' solid mass. She spun apprehensively, weary of being caught and tossed into the tub, her eyes wide, pleading, fearful.

James took firm hold to Ashley's shoulders, his erection pressing close. Her fear elevated to terror, for she knew well his arousal coincided with violence. She had allowed herself to believe he would dismiss her slip, but now knew otherwise. The situation here was unprecedented. She would rather endure his aggressive advance over what hovered so close. The water would blister the entire surface of her skin. For days she'd know discomfort at the mere caress of fabric. Naked even, her bed would be that of torture.

"Dear Ashley," he said. "What frightens you?"

As if you don't know. You sick son of a bitch!

She tossed a nervous glance over her shoulder. "I had no idea you'd come early," she began. "I would've been naked; I promise I would have." She fumbled at his belt with trembling fingers. "You have to know it was unintentional. I'll do whatever you want. Anything. Just, please, don't throw me in there!"

"Ashley." He stilled her hands at his belt. "It isn't my intent to throw you anywhere, and the water isn't as you fear."

She searched his gaze, uncertain. He wasn't beyond treachery; it was his game.

"Go ahead." He turned her gently about, releasing her. "See for yourself."

A wary eye on him, Ashley tested the water with her toes before stepping in and sinking down, sighing contently.

"How is that?" James asked. He retrieved a sponge and perched on the tub's edge.

"It's nice," she whispered, and James soaked the sponge, trickling water over her neck and shoulders. So nice, in fact, it nearly brought her to tears; so long had it been since last she knew such pampering. The sensation was reminiscent of a time and life with a man at whose hand she'd known no fear. She'd become rather exceptional at distancing herself from the harsh world that has become her reality, and James' slow and gentle strokes made it easier to envision that past life. So much so, she started when James broke the silence to inform her he would return shortly, offering up the sponge and standing to leave.

Ashley listened close for his exit, apprehensive with possibilities. Was he setting her up? Anger accompanied the sentiment in that such would have never been a concern with her fiancé, that every distressful emotion she'd come to know had been non-existent. She was certain now; certain of her want only for her fiancé.

The room door's thrown bolt alerted Ashley. She tensed, uncertain what would come. She was always uncertain, as he wanted her to be, as there was no alternative considering his mentality. James entered carrying across his arm a silk, slender cut evening gown, and Ashley sighed audibly, sinking deeper into the tub.

"I'll lay this out for you," James said. "It will go well with the blue slippers you got from Macy's. Take your time and fix your hair. I must make other preparations." He exited the bathroom and only at hearing the room door's engaging lock did she sink deeper in the tub, eyes closed, reliving in her mind ecstatic moments at the hands of her fiancé.

Chapter 13

Trayon, trailing behind a trio of young women–
college students, judging from their conversation –
filed unobtrusively into the nearly filled conference
room. To his right a tanned, auburn-hair librarian in a
beige two-piece stood behind a wooden podium. At
her back, on the backboard and written in bold letters,
was Trayon's full name and the title of his book,
Pleazotic; the reason for which all were gathered. A
collapsible easel bearing a blowup poster of *Pleazotic*
stood to one side of the podium. A table spread with
his personal business cards, copies of *Pleazotic*, and a
couple bottles of water flanked the other.

The librarian spotted him and flashed a smile that he
acknowledged with a slight nod. Instead of
approaching the podium and table, he went in the

opposite direction, strolling past rows of fold-out chairs occupied by men and women of varying age and race. He took a seat near to the last row, placing himself between a black male and a young woman of Asian descent; the woman to his left, the male to his right. He scanned the room and noted with satisfaction no heads turned his direction. The people had no idea the man they were here to see was among them; the reality would change as soon as the librarian saw fit to make a proper introduction.

"Where the hell is he?" Trayon heard a male voice from over his right shoulder.

"Be patient," a second male spoke further from the right.

"I've been patient," replied the first, "and now I'm anxious to hear what this guy has to say. Anxious to even see what he looks like."

"Anxious?" inquired the second.

"A bit curious, maybe," the first person corrected.

"Yeah? Since when?"

"Since two days ago when Jennifer brought home and read the guy's book and suddenly became a Nympho-girl. She was after me half the night."

"You don't sound so thrilled about it," said the second. "I thought you'd be ecstatic considering her usual lack of interest."

"I'm more than ecstatic," admitted the first, "but it's a bit unsettling how a total stranger can push her buttons in ways I've been trying to for years. You know Jenny; she's anything but sexually aggressive. Makes you wonder at the guy responsible."

"Where is she now?"

"She's up near the front. She may be hot for the guy."

"Be nice, Gabriel," admonished the second. "Jenny's a good girl. She deserves better."

"I know, Steve, but it does nothing to ease my concern. And I never even saw the guy."

The young woman of Asian descent turned and spoke to Gabriel. "I'm able to assist with how he looks, if you can't wait. I have with me a book I hope to have him sign. It has his picture, if you care to see?"

"Ah, sure, why not?"

The young woman produced a book from her purse and passed it to Gabriel. Trayon kept his eyes centered, ears attuned.

"The *Mystics of Roth*," Gabriel read the title aloud, examined the book, and flipped open its cover. He read the author's bio before returning the book to its owner. The black male to Trayon's right leaned forward to address the Asian, asking to see the book.

"Sure," the Asian agreed and extended the book past Trayon's chest. The man briefly appraised the book, and as it was being returned to its owner for the second time, Trayon intercepted it.

"May I?" he asked, taking the book and flipping it open. He fished from his pocket a black pen to take to the inside cover.

"Hey wait!" the Asian woman protested. "What are you—?"

Trayon regarded her with mock puzzlement. "Pardon me, but did I not hear you say you wish to have this signed?"

"Oh my God!" the woman started, one hand coming to her breast. "You're—"

"Or, perhaps," Trayon continued as if he hadn't noticed her startled recognition, "you prefer to have it done in red or blue, both of which I do have." He thumbed the pen's head, retracting the ball point and feinted re-pocketing the pen.

"No, wait!" she protested. "You heard correctly. Black is fine!"

He smiled pleasantly, asked her name, inscribed his signature, and handed the book over to her.

"For Malinda," she read aloud his inscription. "Taken by surprise. Trayon Haymon." She beamed at him. "Thanks so much, Trayon. I'm such a fan of yours."

She held up the *Mystics of Roth.* "So when can we expect book two?"

Trayon sighed. "It has only recently been submitted and has to go through the proper channels, and you are the first to have my apology.

"How recent?" she asked.

"Three days."

"Will you honor me with a sneak peek?" Her voice was hopeful. "I mean, can you give me a hint at what's to come?"

"Let's see.... Kendell's medallion will be made more powerful by the God Zektor."

Malinda's eyes went wide. "You mean the God of peace and prosperity? You can't be serious! Whatever are his reasons for doing so?"

"For that you must wait and see."

She smiled broadly. "I'm more eager now than ever! Thanks, again, Trayon. I'm honored."

"The honor is mine, Malinda." Trayon turned in his seat. "Gabriel?" he said, extending a hand to the man who was anxious to see him. "Trayon Haymon."

Gabriel, a Caucasian with dark brown hair in his early twenties, shook the hand extended. "Gabriel Rau."

"Hey, listen." Trayon kept his voice low so as to minimize those who heard. "I could not help but overhear your earlier comment regarding Jennifer. I can offer some insight if you would listen to me."

"I'm all ears, man," Gabriel said with an opened-arm gesture.

"I gather your relationship is monogamous, correct?"

Gabriel nodded.

"With that, I can tell you she didn't choose *Pleazotic* for HIV awareness. I think it's safe to say she recognized the strain in that area of your relationship. I'm sure she isn't as uninterested as you believe her to be. It may be her preference is something other than what you know. She may or may not be conscious of her own preference. She's searching blindly, feeling out. In her own way she's attempting to convey this to you. The fact you're even aware she's read *Pleazotic* confirms this. She has made clear the book's effect.

You must read it now. Dissect it. It's what she wants. "I'll let you in on a little secret. In writing *Pleazotic*, I consulted several women for insight. It's one of the reasons the book is so appreciated by women. Sometimes women want a man to simply know, to simply understand, and they can become frustrated and angry at times when we don't. A woman wants to feel that connection, and when it comes to sex, she must feel that it is all about her. If you do this right she will come to you and/or eagerly anticipate your every advance.

"Ask to read her copy. This will tell her in ways words never could that you hear her cry and you are willing. She will then relax, thus becoming open to discussion. Talk with her. Use the book as reference. Ask her honest opinion about the content therein. You must never be afraid to go there. By 'there' I mean wherever she needs you to go.

"There's a book by Stephanie Ransom, entitled *Her Way*. I strongly suggest you check it out. Jennifer will love you for it– not that she doesn't already. This book is one that women leave lying around while silently praying their man will stumble upon it. Remember this, Gabriel: her pleasure becomes your own. I've spoken more than was my intent here, but I know my words were well taken. The fact you even voiced your concern says you're open to suggestions. You'll do well, Gabe."

Having been silent throughout, his expression blank, Gabriel smiled. "Your bio says nothing about psychology."

Trayon contained his humor. "Understanding character goes a long way. Besides, an author must write with conviction, which entails studies in fields many never suspect. For me psychology just happens to be one of them."

"Ladies and gentlemen," the librarian called from the podium. "May I have your attention please?"

"Well," Trayon addressed Gabriel. "Your curiosity is soon to be sated. The person you've been waiting for will soon be front and center. I hope you gain all you wish in hearing him speak."

Gabriel laughed. "You're something, man, and way more down to earth than I thought you'd be. I've already gained more insight than I ever imagined I would in hearing you speak. No doubt you've saved our relationship. I couldn't stand it if she ever wanted to leave me. Thanks Mr. Haymon." He extended his hand.

Trayon shook it. "No problem. And call me Trayon." "As you know," the librarian announced. "K. D. Hampton sponsors an annual HIV/AIDS awareness conference, bringing to you speakers of great stature from across the continent. This year the staff of K. D. Hampton presents to you a renowned author of fiction and fantasy. He is a native of Savannah, Georgia, and his approach with today's subject is rather unique. Ladies and gentlemen please welcome Trayon Haymon."

The conference room erupted in applause, men and women alike coming to their feet. Heads turned about and towards the entrance as they sought the person introduced. Trayon rose from his seat and headed towards the podium, all but oblivious to the exclamation from those who only now realized he'd been among them for some time. His thoughts were of Gabriel, of how distraught the young man had come across in his anxiety with Jennifer. He cared deeply for the woman; it was evident in his speech, in his tone, and it had weakened Trayon's heart to hear it so prominently, to know the guy harbored a fear of losing her, to know that fear could very much become a reality.

Knowing firsthand the heartache associated with sexual infidelity, Trayon wished never to have such befall another. It was only appropriate to offer what he had. If only it had been something so trivial in the case with Ashley, he thought, and was again reminded of his continued love for the woman. He sighed, distancing the emotion and setting his mind for the current task.

Trayon clasped the librarian extended hand in both his own and planted a kiss on her cheek. She beamed at him, left the podium, and took a seat in the front row.

"Good morning ladies and gentlemen," Trayon spoke as the applause subsided. "Can anyone here tell me the acronym for HIV and AIDS?"

Over half the hands in the room shot up.

"You," Trayon pointed at a young male with wavy blond hair. "The young man in the blue and white Tommy shirt. Stand-up"

The young man stood hesitantly. "HIV stands for human immunodeficiency virus, and AIDS stands for acquired immunodeficiency syndrome."

"That's correct." Trayon said, stepping to one side of the podium and draping his arm over the wooden surface as the young man sat down again. "HIV weakens the immune system; the body's natural defense against illness. By the AIDS stage, the immune system is very weak, no longer able to effectively fight or protect against illness."

He proceeded to inform how the virus is spread, how to prevent and reduce the risk of contracting the disease or possibly transmitting it to others. He covered the symptoms and the effects HIV has on the body as well as how an individual's knowledge can help them treat others who have the virus with understanding. In that a carrier of the virus knows some degree of psychological trauma and shouldn't be shunned in day-to-day activities and casual contact.

Due to *Pleazotic's* erotic focus, Trayon kept the foremost segment of the lecture centered around the various ways of contracting the virus and protection against it, strategically leaving for last the topic of oral sex and intercourse with repetitive reference to his own book.

The lecture concluded with a string of questions from those gathered. Many were shy or reluctant at posing what they felt were embarrassing, awkward, or explicit questions, but they became at ease under Trayon's encouragement, and questions were thrown one after another. Those of which he was curious to hear and pleased to answer.

"Unfortunately," Trayon announced. "My time here is running near to the end. I'll take one more question then close. I will remain a few moments at the table you see here beside me for any who wish to purchase *Pleazotic* or for those who possess a copy and wish to have it signed."

Several hands went up around the room. A woman midways along the rows rose to her feet, hand half raised. Her manner was cool and casual, demanding in that no other had risen unless called upon. Trayon smiled. The woman held in her hand a copy of *Pleazotic*, an index finger inserted between the close pages.

"Yes," Trayon said, pointing to the standing woman and was only then struck by her familiarity. He looked closer even as she lowered her hand, certain of the woman's identity.

"The sexual content of *Pleazotic* is quite graphic," she said. "What made you decide on that approach?"

Trayon looked her over, assessing her attributes where such isn't his habit. She wore grey slacks and a blouse that revealed a more significant bust than he last recalled. Her hair, which once fell past her shoulders, was styled short. While petite during her years in high school, Samira had come full into the voluptuous figure of a woman, more appealing than he'd imagined she'd come to be. He stuttered, flabbergasted; not by the question, but the woman who posed it, instead. She smiled knowingly.

"It's Dramatization versus Narrative Summary." Trayon recovered. "We constantly hear and read things which remind, express, and highlight the importance of protected sex. We are told of the possible consequence, which is more like a Narrative Summary. We comprehend it, but Dramatization shows it to us, bringing greater impact with its delivery. That is my attempt with *Pleazotic*."

Samira, having stood throughout, nodded her satisfaction and sat down again.

"Ladies and gentlemen," Trayon spoke. "I will conclude this session by thanking you all for coming here today. Again, I will remain at the table for those of you who would like to purchase *Pleazotic* and for those who may have a quick question or two. I'm happy to oblige. Also, there are HIV/AIDS awareness booklets on the stand as you exit. I encourage you to take one, if only for the purpose of passing it along. The world is sexually active and so is the virus."

While many got up and made a quiet exit, two-thirds of those gathered formed a line to one side of the room and came forward one by one to purchase *Pleazotic* or to snatch up business cards or bookmarks depicting various titles of his work. With patience he sat, attentive to all who came forth until the room was near empty.

Having said farewell to a couple, Trayon inscribed his signature within the cover of a copy of *Pleazotic*.

"When you're done with that," a feminine voice said to Trayon's bowed head. "I'd like for you to sign this one."

Trayon completed his inscription and sat the book aside, knowing whose face he would encounter before lifting his gaze to the newcomer. His certainty had wavered as the crowd had dissipated with no sign of her, but he'd known she would stop by if only to speak. The idea of her manifesting the way she had only to run off was unappreciated, even considering their relationship isn't what it had been and years had passed since their last encounter. With that, he warmed at hearing her voice.

"Well, hello Samira," he greeted, his smile reflecting his warmth. "I can't tell you how nice it is to see you, and no figure of speech in saying what a pleasant surprise."

Samira offered him her copy of *Pleazotic*, which he accepted, noting her professional manicure and ring-less ring finger. He scribbled his signature on the inside cover and returned the book, giving her an open once over.

"You look absolutely wonderful, Samira."

She smiled, dimples forming at her cheeks. "Thank you, Trayon. You don't look so bad yourself. A bit slimmer than the latest pictures, however. Ashley isn't feeding you?"

Trayon blinked twice, at loss for words.

"Oh my God!" came her hoarse exclamation. "Is that a direct hit?"

"No." His reply was automatic. "I had an accident."

"Yeah?" she teased. "And Ashley had nothing to do with it, right?"

"I crashed my bike and was hospitalized for a second, that's all"

"Oooh," she cooed. "And in denial, too." Her widening smile froze then faded as his expression remained somber. "It's serious, isn't it?" She spoke softly, her hand covering his.

Denial is easy, but recovery is a result of coming to terms with the truth. He looked pointedly past her at the others awaiting their turn with him. "This isn't exactly the place nor the time."

"You're right." She squeezed his hand encouragingly. "How about dinner? We can talk then."

Trayon glanced down at the hand covering his. She was right-handed and yet she'd extended and taken back *Pleazotic* with her left, extending gestures of comfort with the very same hand. She was bound to none and wanted him aware of it. He knew the implication well and considered declining her offer.

Whatever's the problem, Trayon, his mother's words came to mind.... *Somehow you must come to terms with this. You must fix it.* He sighed deep. What better way to start than to accept what was now offered? He met Samira's expectant gaze. "Where?"

She smiled. "I'll wait for you to finish, here, and we'll decide together."

"Sounds nice."

"Good," she replied. "I will leave you to your business." Samira clutched *Pleazotic* to her breast, turned and made for the exit. Trayon gazed after her, caught by the sway of her hips and the fact years had passed since last he'd eyed a woman as he did now. In the fullness of womanhood, he mused, his high school sweetheart had become something beyond beautiful.

Chapter 14

With Richmond as her home, her superior knowledge of the city's geological layout, Trayon had left the choice of what and where for dinner entirely up to Samira; a decision which landed them at Heart and Soul, her favorite soul food restaurant. In its cozy atmosphere the two sat tucked into a corner booth, their order having been served moments earlier.

"One question," Samira said, placing a bare rib bone to her plate in exchange for one heavy with meat. "How in heaven do you know this? I mean, not only that she's mistreated by the guy, or that she is trapped– though I can't begin to fathom how that may be –but you came into this how?"

The inevitable question. Trayon bit attentively at his pig's feet. "It's a bit complicated," he said.

She cocked an inquisitive brow. "Complicated as in you not trusting her as completely as is your claim? That you were a bit suspicious for whatever reason and placed a P.I. on her tail?"

"Samira, No!" His reply was quick. "There was no suspicion and neither was there a private investigator. My trust in Ashley was complete, and had it been as you questioned, the overall effect wouldn't have been as traumatic."

She sipped from her glass of lemonade. "Okay, but that still leaves my question unanswered."

She was even more difficult than he remembered. "Look, Samira. A lie would be far more convincing than the truth here, but a lie isn't what I'm going to tell you. So trust me when I say there was no suspicion on my behalf, no P.I. or anything to that nature. The fact is she cheated. I was taken by surprise with it and the way in which I received the knowledge."

Her face was serious. "And by what way was that?"

Trayon stared incredulously as Samira brought the glass to her lips, drinking deep, her eyes sparkling with something vaguely familiar. The glass came away, lips pursed, dimples hinting at her cheeks. He squinted, caught on, and uttered her name severely.

She laughed then, dimples cutting in deep. The sound was beautiful and so was she. He laughed with her, reminded of their years together in high school.

"Oh, my God," she sobered. You haven't changed one bit in being so damn serious."

"In that respect," he countered. "You are as difficult as ever."

"I don't remember you complaining."

"I don't now. It fits you. Your humor as well."

"That, too, you always said." Her eyes were reminiscent, stirring the onions and gray together with mashed potatoes. "Heavy dramatization. And to think it all began with you writing plays for Ms. Powell. I never understood your focus. God, I can't write like that."

In English and Science she had come to him with all writing assignments. He smiled. "The focus isn't so great these days," Trayon admitted. "And wasn't it the isolation and focus you got fed up with and left, prompting you to seek attention elsewhere?" Her eyes, cast down at her plate, shot up to meet his, incredulity the fix of her countenance.

"Trayon! You know well—" She stopped at his developing smile. "Besides," she continued. "I'm here now."

Tonight? Or did she harbor in mind some prolonged association for them. He sighed, uncertain with regards to either. "It won't work, Samira."

She blinked, her expression blank. "Give me one good reason?"

"I'm not ready, and a lot of my time is dedicated to research, writing, and all that comes with the business that is now my career."

Samira's humor surfaced at that, her dimples cutting deep, and he was again struck by her beauty.

"Need I remind you of my executive position?" she said. "Demanding at times. A strain on a man who requires his woman's extended presence. I believe our careers are compatible."

Trayon shook his head, and Samira pressed her advance, pointing out the elapsed time, that he shouldn't be so distraught considering the circumstances involving the separation.

"Besides," she said. "It's not like you tragically lost someone all loving and faithful." She made deep eye contact with him. "I would understand your need for space and wouldn't look elsewhere for attention."

"Are you insinuating this is what happened with Ashley?" Trayon cut in. "I can assure you, however, she didn't lack attention or anything else for that matter."

"I insinuate no such thing," she said. "Though if what you say is true, one would be curious as to her motive. I meant only that I've been around and I'm ready to settle. Infidelity is something you need not fear from me. I would be ever faithful, patient, all that you need me to be."

"Then what?" he snapped. "Someone comes along and says all the right things, pushes all the right buttons, and then you go and give him all that you swore was mine alone!"

Samira, startled by his tone, recoiled as if physically struck. She set down her fork and reached across the table to clasp his hand in both her own. "Oh, baby," her voice tender with concern. "The wounds *are* deep." She stroked his fingers with her thumbs, her eyes staring compassionately into his.

"People sometimes make the mistake of asking too much too soon," she said. "The result can be one making promises they can't keep. It wouldn't be so with me. Should we not test the water?"

"Well, ah…" Trayon struggled and was spared by his Samsung's staccato vibrations. The signature alert identified the caller. Excusing himself, he answered, "Hello?"

"Trayon?" his mother called.

"Hey, momma."

"Is everything according to plan?" she questioned. Though cheerful, anxiety rode beneath. It sent shivers down his spine. It wasn't so much her stress as it was the reason behind it. The behavior isn't her character and he desperately wanted to know the source of her fear, but now wasn't the time.

"It is and I'm having dinner with a friend." He promised to speak later with her and shortly concluded the call.

Samira reached across the table to take Trayon's hand. "Do we give it a shot?"

For years Trayon had known no woman's touch but Ashley's. His love nullified his desire for any other. He encountered flirtatious women and was extended intimate invitations, but they held no more appeal to him than did a carat to a rabbit. The hand stroking his arm now was both alien and familiar, oddly seductive and mentally arousing. He was curious, though they had known one another intimately. She was slender back then and timid in temperament. The woman who sat across from him now was voluptuous and aggressive, a seemingly promising liaison.

"Okay, Samira." Trayon rose from his seat. "I'm at Star Screen Plaza, on Sunset. Room two, two, five. You know the place?"

She rose with him. "Yeah. A few blocks North of Edgar Allan Poe's Museum."

"You're into authors?" he asked.

"Just one in particular." She smiled. "And I aim to have him in me."

The emphasis wasn't lost. Trayon arched his brows at the thought, and together they walked toward the exit.

Chapter 15

In the hotel suite of Star Screen Plaza, Trayon lay
alone across the queen size bed, his company having
departed moments before. He lay not as a male sated
by the fulfillment and promise of an eager, obliging
woman. Not as a man who felt pride at bringing to a
female the blissful state of orgasmic release. He lay,
instead, a man baffled. A man embarrassed and
flustered with his impotence. He'd had Samira naked
beneath him, inflamed, her hazel eyes burning with a
savage lust rare to women. Her breasts, twin
mountains of sensual flesh, were pressed firm against
him. Her thighs were parted wide, awaiting,
demanding his entry.

"Oh, God," she'd moaned as he'd kissed her neck.
"It's been so long. Oh, so long."

Since the two of them? Or merely her last indulgence? He didn't question, but considering how she seeped with feminine moisture, soaking the sheets on which they lay, he would guess at the latter.

He kissed her everywhere except there, unwilling to perform so intimate and act. She wanted it but seemed to understand his reluctance. She clutched at him while grinding her pelvis hard to his. Her passion was contagious, but affecting him only in mind. She wasn't faking; hers was the body of a woman who desperately wanted that which she clung to. The thought was excruciating, and he wanted nothing more than to slide past the glistening folds of her vulva and into the warm wetness of her woman's center. He ached to possess her in the very way her body demanded.

He could not, however; he was physically flaccid. Never before had he witnessed such longing in a woman– and he could do nothing to accommodate her.

Samira, having had more than her fill of foreplay, sought penetration. She reached between them with eager hands, discovered his condition, and went still. Their eyes met, and her understanding was clear. "No," she whispered, head shaking slowly. "No!" she said more fiercely, the fire fading from her eyes and leaving them cold, dark, and accusing.

Trayon looked away.

"Get up." She spoke through clenched teeth, pushing at his chest.

He rolled onto his back and watched her gather her discarded clothing. She paused at the bedside, pushed her arms through the straps of her bra, and hooked it in place.

"Ashley had no qualms about fucking someone else, so why should you?" She surveyed the room, spotted her panties, and went to snatch them up, aligning them accordingly and thrusting in one foot after another. She squatted and bowed her legs as she worked them up over her hips to where the stretched elastic snapped against her waist as her thumbs slipped free.

"Look, Samira," he said. "I'm sorry–"

She turned on him. "You're absolutely right. A man that's so stuck on a woman who is long gone– one, in fact, who ran off for some more dick –is damn sorry!"

"Samira," he called disappointedly, and she must have heard it in his voice. Her face softened and so did her tone when next she spoke.

"Okay," she said. "I'm sorry. Maybe you didn't deserve that one, but she has you in the very way women want to have their men– I'm envious." She pulled on her slacks and fastened them, sitting down on the bed next to him. "You haven't moved on as you seem to think you have." She ran a hand over his stomach and over his chest. "Some part of you still clings to her. Your inability to perform confirms it." She kissed him long and deep.

"Come to terms with it," she said. "And truly make your decision. You'll wreck yourself otherwise." She pushed away from him and off the bed. "I need a cool shower and it wouldn't do to have it here with you." She finished dressing and left the suite.

Trayon lay alone now, naked, with only the lingering smell of Samira's perfume as a reminder of what could have been. He trailed his hand along the sheets and felt the moisture left by her desire. How was it he couldn't respond to that?

Ashley. For months she'd been physically absent from his life, but she had never been absent in mind. He did cling to her in part. Credence was in the mere fact her possessions remained in place at his home.

Come to terms or wreck yourself, Samira had cautioned. He would have to let go. The consequences were detrimental. Ashley had chosen and so now must he. His sanity, his physical well-being and career depended upon it.

Whatever the problem, his mother's words came to mind. *It's destroying you, and that brings suffering to me... You must fix it, Trayon.*

I don't know what in hell is going on with you, Newberry's angry voice was clear... *You're in breach of contract... You're pushing it buddy!*

Come to terms with it and truly make your decision, Samira's gentle voice was almost a caress. *You'll wreck yourself otherwise.*

Months earlier, when he had first come to Ashley with questions of infidelity, he'd given it much consideration and had taken, what felt to him, the gentlest approach to the subject. She protested her innocence, however, denying what he knew to be true. He'd practically begged her to come clean, but she'd been adamant with her claim of innocence.

"I'll be home tomorrow," she'd said. "And if you really want to have this conversation we'll talk some more then…"

He was furious, the statement having revealed a facet of Ashley he hadn't known. A daunting discovery, and for that he wanted her nowhere near him. She appeared blissfully ecstatic in James' arms. Almost as ecstatic as she had been at home with him. For the grace of God he couldn't figure what James had to offer that he himself could not provide.

Naked still, Trayon rolled onto his stomach, the question of Ashley's treachery as elusive now as it had been from the beginning. Unbidden came Samira's earlier plea for his hand.

I would understand your need for space, she had said to him. *And wouldn't look elsewhere for attention.*

Are you insinuating this is what happened with Ashley? he shot back. *I can assure you, however, she didn't lack attention or anything else for that matter.*

I insinuate no such thing. Though if what you say is true, one would be curious as to her motive. I meant only that I've been around and I'm ready to settle. Infidelity is something you need not fear from me. I would be ever faithful, patient, all that you need me to be.

Trayon sat upright. Though reluctant to swallow, and opposed to her chosen method, he understood now that Ashley's treachery wasn't so treacherous.

Engaged to be married, Trayon had known his share of women and was certain of his want only for Ashley in matrimony. While she, on the other hand, had known no other. Fiercely loyal, she would hold true to her vows and would come to marriage with nothing short of certainty, with no sacrifice to happiness.

Blinded by a male's pride, Trayon could neither accept nor agree, but there was only one way for Ashley to gain that certainty.

I'll be home tomorrow, she had said. *And if you really want to have this conversation, we'll talk some more then.*

He hadn't given her a chance to come clean. Instead, he'd forbidden her return. She would have confessed had he truly wanted her to, but such then hadn't been his interpretation.

Trayon sighed, falling back to his pillow and staring at the ceiling. The understanding he'd wanted for so long was his now. The hurt remained and his anger wasn't the least diminished. Ashley had seemed unconcerned by his rejection, carrying on merrily with James until the visions revealed the drastic change in their relationship; the beatings, forced sex, her imprisonment.

The visions of late, however, revealed no further abuse nor forced sex, though she remained confined to her room. The current proceedings were strange. There was no intercourse, but James would, with her consent, caress her fervorously, before making his exit and locking the door. The actions were uncharacteristic of the man. He wanted her, surely, but didn't oblige his desire. There was a missing element to the madness and Trayon had given heavy scrutiny to the visions for some clue as to what, as he did now with the memory of such.

It seems the man was attempting to placate Ashley, as if he again wanted her trust and favor. Was it the man's attempt to seduce her? Did he harbor some misguided hope of her again knowing a desire for him? The man's true preference was sexual oppression; he was more passionate about it than he was with the gift of a woman's giving. If he managed to win her over, it would only be to crush her again, leading her to a comfort zone before blindsiding her with his attack; so was the man's nature.

Trayon was struck by a second factor, rolling onto his side, cradling his head in the crook of his arm, clutching his stomach and suppressing a groan; the revelation entirely too much for him.

It's destroying you, his mother's words came to mind.

You're pushing it buddy! Newberry's angry voice cut in.

Come to terms with it, Samira had cautioned. *You'll wreck yourself otherwise.*

Trayon pulled his knees closer to his chest, facing the reality of what had to be. He knew now his decision, what it must be. He had to let go.

Chapter 16

Rosalyn's morning routine began with the mundane activity of dressing and the leisure preparation and consumption of an early breakfast before leaving home a quarter past eight to open the shop for business. *CNN* was viewed throughout breakfast, the news provider being one of the first in bringing to the people the most extraordinary and sometimes life changing events from around the globe.

While U.S. Citizens would undoubtedly mark the Boston bombing and Hurricane Katrina as the most catastrophic and terrifying events in the nation's last decade, others around the globe would attest to the earthquake in Haiti or Japan's tsunami as the most daunting disaster. Rosalyn would concede they were all heart-stopping and catastrophic events, but paled in comparison to the excruciating sense invoked by the unfolding events in the state of Virginia this morning.

Rosalyn sat now before an all but forgotten plate of hash browns, eggs, and bacon, her gaze transfixed on the dining room's mounted Plasma TV. The horizontal text alerted viewers to the breaking news as the anchorman addressed the matter with nothing more enlightening than what was offered by the strolling text. Her heart leapt and beat even faster as the anchorman announced the arrival of their field reporter on the scene, that they were now going live.

On screen, the frame stilled then flipped to a woman with solemn green eyes that reflected none of the trepidation associated with the current scenario.

"This is Renea Duckworth with *CNN*, reporting to you live from Richmond Virginia, where only moments before, a Southwest airliner exploded just seconds after leaving the runway. You can see behind me what remains of flight four-thirty-one after that fiery detonation."

The camera panned away to zoom in on a cordoned section of black top on which gathered an array of vehicles. Firemen and officers alike bustled about the littered runway in a coordinated effort amidst twisted metal and debris which vaguely hinted at its previous construction.

"There were one-hundred and fifty-two passengers aboard flight four-thirty-one," the reporter went on, "and so far there are no survivors. Authorities have yet to determine the cause of the explosion, although there is the question of terrorism…"

Rosalyn's gaze was absent. Considering the mangled fuselage, there wouldn't be any survivors. Catastrophic indeed, for flight 431 had been Trayon's scheduled flight to California.

From the moment her son had confessed to visions, Rosalyn had known he had strayed from the path, that God was calling for his return and such should not be ignored. The reality of which had shaken the depths of her soul. That he returned to God was imperative, and time was winding quickly away. Her belief in God was firm, but Trayon's revelation served as re-enforcement to her faith, reminding her that God was indeed all powerful, his way mysteriously beyond the norm. It brought to mind the mantra Reverend John called upon his church members to recite at every sermon: "With God, nothing's impossible. I can do all things through Christ who strengthens me."

Rosalyn had felt Trayon's peril as if it were her own, ominously pressing in for days. Just last night it had risen to a peak, weighing in heavily and driving her near to panic. Trayon's fate at that moment, she knew, was precariously balanced by some fathomless factor. She had prayed, and the weight was lifted. The comforting hand of solace fell upon her, bringing sleep and the certainty all was well with her son, that he'd chosen correctly, had rectified or adhered to the Lord's will, having found grace with God.

Now this; his flight mangled and strewn about the runaway with no survivors. She was baffled and stricken by what the news conveyed, having gone to sleep utterly convinced of her son's welfare, as if God himself had assured her. He had, she was certain, yet there was no denying the news. Her pulse pounded hard in her ears as her heart fluttered unprecedentedly. She was close to hyperventilating, and in silently questioning God's reassurance the previous night, the reality of the matter suddenly hit home: It had been the redemption of her son's soul for which assurance had come, not his life.

Rosalyn regained control of her breath. The pounding in her ears subsided as the rate of her heart slowed to something less than erratic. The pain at such a loss was tremendous, but it was God's will, and she could only accept. Though lost to her in life, God had provided her with the blessing of knowing she would reunite with her son in heaven. With a heavy heart, she took up her fork and went back to her breakfast. She would need all her strength to carry on.

"With God, nothing's impossible," she recited the mantra aloud. "I can do all things through Christ who strengthens me."

CHAPTER 17

Over the burning flames of twin candles in holders of shining silver, Ashley stared James directly in the eyes, searching for some clue as to how it would end. He had come to retrieve her from the bedroom after leaving her to bathe, finding her beautifully garbed in the evening gown and slippers, hair styled to perfection.

Having grown unaccustomed to seeing her so elegantly dressed, James was more than taken by her appearance, staring hungrily, eliciting her fear of being ravished on the spot. Where once the idea was flattering, she found it repulsively alarming now. He merely appraised her beauty, however, lead her downstairs into the dining room where he courteously pulled out her chair and beckoned her to sit, sliding her close to a table topped with southern fried chicken, cornbread, a tuna casserole, a large bowl of salad sprinkled with bacon bits, French and Ranch dressing, a pitcher of sweet tea, a bottle of champagne, and glasses to accommodate either.

The table seated six with fork, knife, plate, and spoon at every place mat, though only the two were present, opposite one another on the broad sides of the oval table.

She watched him closely now, scanning for answers. His face was a boyish mask of innocence, but the wolf lurked beneath. The night could end savagely and she quivered with the thought, hating the abuse, the forced sex and the response he demanded to it.

James filled his champagne glass and offered to fill hers, but she declined.

"Perhaps some tea?" he asked, exchanging the bottle for the pitcher, filling the appropriate glass.

"What's the point in all of this?" Ashley spoke abruptly, waving a hand at him, herself, and the table before them. The fiery spirit he'd made so many attempts to break and snuff out, flared and bled through with her question.

"You've been mistreated, here, lately," he said.

Mistreated? Is that what you call it?

He hung his head, "I'm sorry."

Ashley picked up her fork and stirred her tuna, taking a forkful to her mouth as James sipped his champagne.

"I want back your true passion, Ashley. The fire with which you'd first given yourself to me."

Passion? Ashley nearly choked. *I'll show you passion, alright, but never again in that fashion.*

Although his sex had been nice once, it wasn't as electrifying as it always had been with her fiancé. There was no substitute; the current brought flames to sex. That current, she realized, was love, and James held none for her. She was to him a mere possession to control, dominate, and to do with as he so felt.

I lost out because of you, you stupid son of a bitch. Then you turn out to be a demented bastard in need of psychiatric help!

Ashley's grip tightened on her fork.

Passion?

It was her want to spring across the table and stab him in the throat.

I'll show you passion!

The thought seemed simple enough and easily carried out— as had others before— but she was physically inferior and could not beat him with her strongest attempt. She paid dearly in every event, and the night he had choked her near to death is what had really shaken her defiance. She would never forget that night, and the unbidden memory fueled her anger. She would love to show him passion, and someday she would. It couldn't be so now, however, for it would only result in another failed attempt.

Ashley slackened her hold on the fork with a conscious effort, taking a mouth full of tuna. She took another, swallowed quickly and went for the chicken. It was delicious and she welcomed the treat, having had nothing more than fruits, snack-cakes, and sandwiches served to her for weeks. She broke off a piece of cornbread, stuffed her mouth, and washed it down with tea, conscious of how he watched. His statement was untrue, she knew. He cared nothing for sharing true passion. True passion for him was abuse, oppression, and rape.

"How is it?" James asked.

"Excellent. Considering my diet of late, though, you could have served me barbecue rat and I'd have found it equally nice." Something flickered across his face, too brief to name.

"Speaking of which," he said. "I have decided to take a few days' vacation, and tomorrow I'd like to have lunch with you at Clyde Cooper's"

"Legendary," she responded. "Raleigh's oldest barbecue shack."

He frowned. Whether at her familiarity or the manner in which she'd spoken, she couldn't say. She eyed him, once more searching his face for some clue as to what was truly to come.

"What do you think of Ocracoke Island?" he asked.

"Never heard of it." She bit into her cornbread.

James smiled, sipped his champagne, and looked winsomely at her. "It's one of North Carolina's barrier islands. No cars allowed, and ponies run wild over a hundred- and sixty-acre expanse. I can tell you more but I'd rather you see for yourself." She stared blankly.

His smile broadened. "It will be nice."

Ashley nearly smiled at him. She loved horses. Though ponies were something smaller, they were no less beautiful. She visualized coats of white, gray, brown, and black; untamed, wild, and free… Her eyes narrowed. "You're one evilly sick bastard," she snapped at him. "Why would you tease me like that?"

He appeared taken aback. "I'm not teasing, Ash. I truly intend to take—"

"I know well what you intend. Of course you'd take me. I'd see them wild, careless, and free; total contrast to how you have me here, to what I must return to. You'd enjoy being there beside me knowing the effect the sight bears on my soul.

''Then again, maybe you have no intentions of taking me to neither Clyde's nor this island you speak of.

Who's to say this whole day isn't part of one of your twisted games and you're only seconds away from doing what you've been doing to me for months now!" She glared at him across the table.

From the hall upstairs came the deep bong of the grandfather clock marking off the hour. Ashley counted nine. Dinner would soon end and she would be taken to bed.

"Give me that." She gestured at the champagne bottle, and James handed it over after topping off his glass. Filling her own, she drank it down to half and filled it again, uncertain of James' intent. Here, tonight, he'd been exceptional, but if the past is any indication, savagery was soon to follow. How, though, would he bring it? The more she contemplated it, the more tempted she was to fly across the table at him with her fork.

Ashley fed herself from the serving of greens and chased it down with half a glass of champagne. The repercussions of such an attack kept her in check. That and the possibility he may want only for sex, leaving her alone thereafter. She felt the alcohol taking hold and welcomed its effect. Her aim was desensitization against any beatings and/or his version of love making. She preferred the latter over the former and detested both.

As an attorney, Ashley had known several cases of abuse but never had she foreseen herself as a victim. She wished to be free of this nightmare, to know reality in co-existence with her fiancé. He'd been nothing other than loving to her, something she understood and cherished more now than ever. He'd given her all that James had stolen. He was perfect in ways uncommon in men; understanding, compassionate, considerate– until that day. He'd failed her when it mattered most. He'd wronged her for a wrong that wasn't so much a wrong.

Marriage is a lifelong commitment and vow she would hold honorably. With that, wasn't she allowed to be certain before committing to it? To be sure of her happiness with him? Would he be so selfish to deny her that right?

A fair man, as he calls himself, must be fair in all things. In this he'd failed; he'd cast her aside while calling her a liar and cheat, none of which is true in light of the whole. He'd denied her the chance to explain, forbidding her return. She questioned his love and understanding as a result. Were they as he'd claimed, his response would've been anything but what it had been. He was too knowledgeable in the ways of people to not know or to not suspect the truth behind her act.

"I'll be home tomorrow," she had said to him. "And if you really want to have this conversation, we'll talk some more then."

But he had cut her off, suggesting such would have never happened had she truly loved him. She did love him and it had to happen. Love doesn't stifle one's desire nor their curiosity. She had found herself more than curious about James, having never realized that such could ever be with her for anyone other than her fiancé. It shook her foundation and threatened her world as she knew it. She'd indulged James for the knowledge of certainty, to know the touch of another, whether she could faithfully embrace the vows of marriage thereafter.

Her indulgence was nice, and she had been passionate about it. Even so, the act could not match that shared with her fiancé. Having known the experience, she could return home to him and take her vows with certainty, but he'd forbidden her return. The thought upset her, for his decision bespoke selfishness. She understood his anger, what must be his feelings of betrayal. Yet she expected better of him. He was no ordinary man. The vows of marriage were sacred. She had yet to make such and sought only certainty. It was her right.

Ashley ate in silence with James occasionally breaking the silence to speak on their trip to come, ensuring her delight with the marvels of Ocracoke. He came off as sincere in his desire to have her witness the gem, but could she dare hope? It wasn't the trip which held such appeal, but the reprieve itself; a welcome change in what has been for months. It would increase her chances of survival.

Ashely knew James' potential for murder, and she feared he may come to feel he couldn't release her and escape prosecution. The incurred charges of the last month would earn him life in prison. He'd made the mistake of releasing his last victim and it had come back to haunt him. He wouldn't make that mistake a second time. Her death would simply nullify the threat…

And suddenly she knew. She had feared it, had considered it a possibility, but knew it now as one knew day followed night. The idea was beyond dread and terror. It was indeed the grand finale of doom, and it would take place at Ocracoke. She viewed it with clarity; he would stage her death as an accident. There was no doubt about it.

His leniency and gentle caress of late was no attempt to win back passion; they were precautions against forensics. He wanted nothing untoward in the autopsy report. The lunch at Clyde's would serve only as a front to those observing them as a loving couple. Her heart raced as the pieces came together. She began to panic, to know fear as she'd never known it before.

Ashley had no intention of letting him kill her off, but how could she stop it? She had no idea what he planned and if she refused to accompany him, he would simply improvise. Forty-eight hours. She would die in forty-eight hours if she didn't kill him first or find a way to change his mind without tipping her hand. She would try at persuasion, for any physical attempt would result in a failed attack and would undoubtedly bring about an even earlier demise.

With trembling fingers, her plate now clear, Ashely reached for the champagne bottle and topped off her glass. She drank deeply with fingers splayed possessively around the bottle.

James frowned. "Ashley, dear, I know your intent but it isn't necessary."

"Excuse me?" she said, alarmed but offering him her most innocent look. She couldn't let on what she suspected, for even his suspicion could prove detrimental.

"I know your drinking habit," he said to her. "It is next to none, yet you've sat throughout dinner and have nearly consumed an entire bottle alone. Now why is that? I presume it to be your want to pickle yourself against what you fear you may endure tonight."

Ashley sighed inwardly. That had been so initially, but she drank now to steady her nerves against a far deadlier threat.

"I can assure you," he went on. "That you will endure no mistreatment tonight or any other. However, I do long for you, Ashley, and if you will extend the invitation to your bed, you will find me tender and loving."

She didn't want him tender nor loving. She didn't want him near her. She wanted to be away from him and the madness that has become her world. She stared blankly at him over the candle flames. She would submit if he came to her, but she would extend him no invitation without good reason. As it stood, there was no reason at all.

"There is dessert in the fridge," he continued as if undaunted by the silence. "Cinnamon crusted cheesecake. I'll fetch a slice, if you like?"

She was of a mind to decline but thought better. "That would be nice."

James left the dining room and returned shortly carrying two slices of cheesecake on ceramic saucers. One of which he deposited before her, taking the other for himself. He asked her opinion regarding the treat, and she was surprised at his boast of having made it from scratch.

Ashley ate slowly, knowing the completion of desert would conclude dinner. Though he'd said there'd be no mistreatment, there was no guarantee he'd hold true to that. More so was her concern with his plans for her. She was marked for death and it made sense to place it at Ocracoke, according to his vacation plans, but she couldn't be certain. What would stop him from killing her that very night? What might he have planned?

Having finished dessert, James cleared the table and blew out the candles. Like a young prince curtsying a princess, he extended a hand to Ashley, leading her from the dining room and up the stairs in the direction of her bedroom.

Ashley was heavy with a sense of alarm. Having paused near her open bedroom door, she was again under James' hungry gaze. With hands at her shoulders, he didn't ask for permission; he simply covered her mouth with his. She knew his preference, and was no longer required to oblige him in that manner, but she wouldn't take that risk; she opened her mouth to him.

Ashley's chances at survival were feminine persuasion. James was weak for her, and she would exploit that weakness. She relaxed, molding her body to his, and with a play at reluctance, she slid her arms around his neck. He groaned into her mouth, his tongue delving deep, exploring vigorously and meeting with hers. His hands moved along her shoulders, down and around her waist. Alarmed, she stiffened abruptly and broke the kiss.

James was breathless. His expression was that of hunger, confusion, and dismay. "W.... What's wrong, Ashley?" he said.

Her alarm was genuine, but the true reason couldn't be known. "Surprisingly," she thought quickly. "I find myself responding to you… But I fear what this may become."

He nodded. "I know, and I promise it will be as it were in the beginning." He caressed her cheek with the back of his fingers. "If only you will permit me."

She had him now. His lust would be her salvation. She gave him a shy, almost embarrassed smile.

"If you kiss me elsewhere as you did just now, I'd be more than willing."

"Then it shall be as you wish," he said. He released her and she went quickly into the room. She had her gown off, the covers turned, and was in the bed with only panties and bra by the time the door was locked, the lights were dimmed, and he was at her bedside. He stripped hurriedly and fell on top of her.

Ashley's nerves were on end; the moment of truth was near. James kissed her while sliding his hands behind her back. The straps to her bra snapped loose and he tossed the garment aside, caressed and kissed her breast, down further to her stomach. His tongue probed the circle of her naval, and as his fingers hooked her panty line, she drew up her knees and planted her feet to the mattress, lifting her hips for him to remove the lacy fabric. Her feet came up as he worked the material below her knees, past her ankles and feet, legs parting for his kiss.

A nervous quiver ran throughout her body; the moment of truth was closer still. He trailed his tongue from her knee to her thigh and very near to her center. He repeated the action with her left leg, parting her with his thumbs, exposing her to the warmth of his breath.

She squirmed and placed her hands to his head, encouraging him to proceed.

James' mouth made contact and she gasped, stroking the back of his neck with one hand, reaching under the pillow with the other to curl her fingers around the handle of a steak knife. The moment of truth. She'd taken the blade from the table's setup as James had gone for dessert, and he'd come close to discovering it hidden beneath her gown just outside the bedroom. From table to bedroom had been nerve racking. She knew the consequence if unsuccessful, but what choice did she have? Death in two days, this very night, or she could dispatch him and win free.

Ashley's breath came faster, deeper, but as no result of the oral stimulation provided by James. She stroked his neck with one hand, marking the target, clutching the knife under the pillow with the other. The oral stimulation continued, and to it she paid no attention. Her focus had to be total, her aim true. She withdrew the knife and eased it ever so carefully in the air above his head. She trembled with anxiety and fear, for her intent was murder and she would have but a single shot. Her goal was to plunge the blade between the vertebrae and sever the spinal cord; instant paralyses and death.

Ashley examined the knife in the dim light, carefully twisting the handle until the flat of the blade was facing her, the tip pointing down. She could afford no mistake now and wanted the best angle of penetration. She felt none of the satisfaction and passion she'd imagined she would have at enacting revenge. This wasn't vengeance for her. It was only a means of survival, a necessity. She was indeed reluctant but compelled by the life or death scenario; him or her. He'd forced this confrontation, and it wasn't in her interest to fail. Here is the moment of truth.

Ashley placed a firm hand to the back of James' head. "That's it," she said, her voice strained with tension. "Right there. Right there." With tremendous force, throwing everything she had behind it, she brought the knife down toward the mark. Maybe it was the sound— inaudible to her— or he may have felt the lurch of every muscle in her body and knew it did not correspond with orgasm or the stimulation he provided, but at the blade's descent, the hand to his head met drastic opposition. Not vertically, for that would have brought his immediate demise, but to one side, instead, his face slamming against her inner thigh.

The blade missed his jugular by mere centimeters, plunging into the mattress with an audible split of fabric and the scrape of metal as it lodged within the coiled springs. He was on her quick, pinning her body beneath his, squeezing her throat.

There was rage in his eyes, murderous rage, and she knew she was going to die, that she would be dead in a matter of seconds. He backhanded her hard across the face, splitting the inside of her jaw; blood leaked into her mouth.

"I knew you would attempt something like this if given the opportunity," he said. "I could see you envisioning it. You nearly snapped the fork in two, so tight was your grip. I had something extraordinary planned for you, but I'll gladly improvise. I'm going to fuck you good, Ashley, as has been my want for some time now. You should enjoy it because this will be your last. This time you won't come back."

Ashley saw black and red dots. They bled together and became mostly black, blotting out her sight of reality. She was slipping away, and could offer no opposition to the way she was pinned. She couldn't scream, speak, or breathe. Even if she could, what would be the sense? Any plea would fall on deaf ears. Any scream would go unanswered. She was left alone with wild thoughts of panic, with the notion of rapidly falling away. The darkness grew thick, terrifying in what it indicated. She could only will herself to remain conscious, not to slip under, for her mind to stand firm against what he forced upon her.

Her will was strong, more so with added desperation, but it was nothing without the proper elements which sustained the mind and focused the will; the oxygen and blood in which he deprived her of. Down the hall the grandfather clock marked off the hour, the sound a chilling toll of death. The darkness continued to close until there was only a pinpoint of light. Her final thoughts were those of her fiancé. She loved him and ached to be with him, but he, with his male pride and selfishness, had left her in the hands of the beast.

By whatever means her fiancé had acquired the knowledge of her infidelity, she couldn't help but wonder if he would have left her to suffer the current fate had he been privy to it as well. In her mind she screamed long and loud. A scream derived from anger, despair, and a sense of betrayal. She had acted out of necessity to ensure both their happiness. She had wanted only to know! And for that he had scorned her. In her mind she screamed again. It echoed strangely; a splintering crash before fading off to silence, dying along with the pinpoint of light…

Chapter 18

Trayon, with escalated breathing and a quickened pulse, paused outside the door to Ashley's prison. Only seconds ago he'd kicked in the front door under the ringing cover of the grandfather clock, praying to God the repetitive bong concealed the crash of forced entry. Ultimately familiar with the house's layout by way of visions, he advanced rapidly through the halls and up the stairs to the master bedroom. Finding it empty, he'd raced down the hall to where he stood now, .38 revolver in hand.

Trayon was aware of the home's ADT security system and knew the access code as well, but had purposely left the system active. Immediately upon entry he'd taken the phone off the hook, leaving no opportunity for an ADT representative to call and verify the home's security. He wanted the authorities alerted, wanted their presence at the house; the ending here was in question. He glanced at his watch, tracking the elapsed time since entry. ADT would have the signal now, and the authorities should be on their way. He couldn't wait for them, however. He sensed Ashley's mortal danger and wouldn't delay another second.

Ear to the door, he listened. Silence came to him and his quickened heart skipped a beat, racing faster. Silence spelled disaster. Clutching the revolver tightly and praying the rusted piece was in working order, he reared back and kicked the door.

A formidable prison and barrier from within, the roomdoor splintered at the jamb, flew in on its hinges, and Trayon was across the threshold even as it crashed back against the wall. In one swift motion he switched the lights from dim to bright and pointed the pistol to where he knew the bed to be– and nearly choked.

James was on top of Ashley with both hands around her throat, and she was still beneath him. Eyes wide, the man's jaw dropped at the intrusion.

"Get off of her, now!" Trayon croaked. His hand trembled as he cocked the hammer. The gun was a bit rusted and he had doubts regarding its ability to fire. He had purchased the weapon from an old taxi driver shortly after his arrival in Raleigh. After last night's revelation, he'd struggled endlessly with the notion of abandoning his early morning flight to California in exchange for a later one to North Carolina. The taxi driver was more than suspicious at Trayon's inquiry in regards to a firearm, and later reluctant, but with the offer of three times its value, the guy had parted with his personal piece.

"I don't know what you're up to," the taxi driver had said. "But I'm going to have to report it lost or stolen to protect my own hide."

Trayon had never fired a gun before and had prayed to God he wouldn't have to this night, but seeing James as he was now with Ashley took all his control not to pull the trigger. He shook with fury. All the love and affection he once felt for Ashley was born again; only it had never died, had only been smothered by hurt, anger, and betrayal. He knew shame for leaving her the way he had. The idea he may have come too late was mind-boggling. What in God's name had he been thinking?

James made no move to comply. Whether immobilized, or he'd simply mistaken Trayon's trembling hand and choked demand as a sign of fear and was attempting to try him as a result, was impossible to tell. Whichever, words weren't sufficient and Trayon had few to spare.

He squeezed the trigger and the cocked hammer leapt forward. The gun resounded loud within the confines of the room, bucking in his grasp as fire exploded from the barrel. The round punched a hole in the far wall near James' head.

He flinched and cringed all at once, tucking his head while snatching his hands away from Ashley's throat, raising them high. Trayon sighed inwardly. He hadn't been sure of the weapons functionality and was grateful it worked accordingly.

"The next one," Trayon's voice was deadly, calm. "Will go where the first should have gone. I've seen everything you've done to her. All I need is just the smallest excuse to blow you away. So don't try me!" His voice had risen with the last sentence and was lowered again as he spoke next. "On second thought, feel free." He walked forward, weapon trained on James' forehead. He was bluffing with regards to executing the man. Though angry, he wouldn't kill James in cold blood, although he'd nearly done so a moment ago. However, he would shoot if the man proved sly in action.

Trayon, looking from James to Ashley's still figure, halted at the bedside. "Get up," he instructed James, gesturing for him to step aside, turning his attention to Asheley. Was she alive and merely unconscious or…. He couldn't finish the thought. He wanted to touch her, to kiss her awake, but he dare not attempt such with James standing within arm's reach. With that, he instructed James to move to the wall and to lay on the floor.

James moved to comply, and Trayon dismissed the man, turning again to Ashley. Was that the shallow rising of her chest? A twitching finger? Hopeful, he bent close to inspect. She was breathing!

James dropped low. The sudden movement caught Trayon's attention and he pulled hard on the gun to bear on the man's descending head. James spun with his descent, his arm arcing out, a steak knife clutched in his fist. Trayon cocked back the hammer, pulling his arm down faster, harder, his finger squeezing the trigger. James completed his spin, burying the knife in Trayon's thigh. The gun fired. The shot went over James' head and into the floor.

Trayon cried out, the blade sending raw tendrils of fiery pain coursing through his thigh and calf like currents of molten lava. Leg numb and unable to support his weight, he toppled backwards. He fumbled the gun, his finger losing their grip as if they, too, were numb. He understood his mistake and knew his peril even as he fell. His head connected hard with the carpeted floor, and the plush material did nothing to cushion the blow. His vision flashed black with streaks of bright blue/white that dissipated to pixels as he clung to consciousness.

James pounced on him, a wolf's intent to kill off the wounded. He grasped the embedded knife and came down with a lateral forearm to Trayon's throat. Trayon raised both hands to fend off the attack. James countered by twisting the knife, and Trayon's roar of agony was cut to a strangled gurgle as one hand went to govern James' handling of the knife, leaving the weaker left to regulate the crushing arm at his throat.

James was methodical in his attack, calculating every move while anticipating the counter, preparing for yet another. Trayon couldn't possibly repel the mounting weight behind James' pressing arm. He was losing ground, the pressure at his throat increasing by the second. He had to act fast, for the man's arm was close to locking in place, and he understood all too well the results of such. He had to gain advantage with a move James wouldn't suspect nor anticipate, therefore, could not easily counter. He knew the move, and it would test his own endurance, however, but there were no alternatives.

Trayon braced himself, relinquished his hold on the knife, and thrust his hand down quickly between them. Unsurprisingly, James twisted the knife the second Trayon's hand was free of it. Trayon cried out, squeezing the man's testicles. James howled in pain and wrenched violently on the knife. It was, Trayon knew, the man's counter in nullifying the attack, but he wouldn't succumb to it, nor would he relent; he fought for his life. Stifling his scream and gritting his teeth,

Trayon applied more pressure to the man's scrotum, his intent, to crush the man's sack in his grasp, sending a silent message that he was in control and had the upper hand.

Message received, James made a hasty attempt to roll away. Trayon, having none of that, went with him, maintaining his grip while solidifying a position on top. James wrenched the blade from Trayon's thigh.

The flow of blood increased, and from this Trayon knew an artery had been torn or severed. The pain was excruciating, but not so much as that which came as the knife was brought up and lodged fiercely into his armpit. Here, also, the knife was twisted, James forcing the metal deep, slicing muscles and tendon, connecting with bone. Though agonizing, the pain was brief, for the entire whole of Trayon's arm went suddenly numb as if the blade had exterminated every nerve ending therein. He could literally feel nothing about his arm and could only acknowledge it by sight.

The quickening and heavy pounding of his heart was futile compensation for blood loss. He felt nothing as the blade was withdrawn and tossed aside. The diminished effect of his arm was reflected in James' eyes. They were less dark, having lost their fury. The man smiled, triumphantly, reached between them and meticulously plucked the nerveless fingers away from his crotch, seemingly enjoying the act while observing Trayon's mounting fear.

Trayon's strength bled with his blood and he could offer no true resistance, but James' assured sense of victory supplied the means to make an effort. He marshaled his depleted energy, made a fist with a knuckle extended and punched down hard at James throat. The blow would crush his windpipe, and there was no counter for that. The man would suffocate and die. The idea was accompanied with a silent plea for God's forgiveness as his fist sped towards the target.

James intercepted Trayon's wrist, halting the fist just centimeters away from his throat. His eyes turned dark with fury, comprehending Trayon's intent. He twisted Trayon's wrist, snatched and locked him into a bear-hug, rolling effortlessly, pinning his arms to the floor. He gripped his throat with both hands and squeezed menacingly. "How about I administer to you a manual version of the same treatment?"

Once again Trayon had underestimated the man. As he could not, neither could James stand to lose. How could he have thought the man would be anything less than ferocious in defending his life? James was the more savage by nature, a stronger fighter. In hand to hand, Trayon had never stood a chance. He had thought the advantage was his in clutching the man's groin, and had assumed the man's roll as an attempt to flee. It had, instead, been another counter/attack.

Trayon admired the man's strength and mental capacity in having rational thoughts and formidable tactics under duress. He had certainly underestimated the man and was now dying as a result, suffocating and bleeding, unable to lift a finger to prevent it. Like his arm, his body went numb and the light of his vision faded to black. His final thoughts were of Ashley; how he loved her; how he had failed her; how he had labeled her callous and inconsiderate when it was he who had been both and more; how he would die and she'd suffer a similar fate as a result.

Chapter 19

Total darkness.... Heavy silence.... Ashley became increasingly aware of both, where moments before there had been neither; she had known only void, a timelessness empty of silence and darkness, empty of physical awareness and thought. She was surrounded by them now; the darkness and silence. She seized at either, for both were more than what had been. Awareness expanded to memory and she knew moments prior to the void. It was first confusing in that the void seemed, upon exiting, an all-encompassing eternity of nothingness, then frightening as the memory brought the full scope of what had come to pass.

James had rendered her unconscious once before and she had simply dreamt throughout, regaining consciousness with him violating her sexually.

Ashley was conscious now, but this was different; silent, dark, and absolutely no sense of the physical. She could only classify her current state as death, and it set her fright to panic. Something audible penetrated the silence and caught her attention: a muffled explosion, a cry; the two entwined as one. The noise was faint, having traveled a great distance to reach her, manifesting in the darkened silence a portal to which she extended herself, latching onto the sound as if it had rungs, sliding her awareness along the longitudinal waves, tracing them back to the origin from which they had come.

The darkness would not hold her. The silence thinned, more akin to quiet. Her awareness broadened and she became conscious of her physical anatomy. The darkness became less dark; a rising sun behind closed curtains.

Comprehending her return from the brink of death, Ashley cracked open her eyelids and was greeted by the familiar surroundings of her prison. She groaned inwardly and wondered whether she truly preferred life over death.

There was no sign of James, but she wasn't alone in the room. Panting, grunts, and labored breathing was audible, bringing her wearily upright. He had promised to make it permanent, so what now was his intent? The door sat open on its hinges; an uncommon occurrence if ever. Under close scrutiny she observed the busted jamb and was utterly perplexed by it.

Movement caught her attention and she turned to it. She'd questioned whether her fiancé would leave her to suffer her fate if he was privy to the knowledge. Her heart soared with the answer. At the same time, it made her question whether she'd truly awakened to reality. For as many times as she'd wished and prayed for it, she'd known in her heart the probability was zero, and yet there was her fiancé on the floor and locked into a fierce battle with James. Transfixed, she watched the proceedings.

James was hunkered down over her fiancé with a forearm hard pressed into his throat, simultaneously clutching an embedded knife in his thigh. Her fiancé had a hold to the knife as well, preventing his assailant from inflicting further damage while attempting to check the crushing arm at his throat. James dropped his weight. Her fiancé's hand withdrew from the knife and shot down between them. He screamed, and James howled, wrenching violently at the knife.

James rolled away. Her fiancé went with him, coming out top. He groaned as James wrenched the knife from his leg, blood-soaked trousers leaking through to the floor. The groan became a cry when James jammed the knife into her fiancé's armpit, twisting and working the handle before setting the blade aside as if it was of no further use.

The triumphant expression he wore as he reached, just as casually, between them was one she'd witnessed on several occasions after he'd beaten her into submission or had successfully countered one of her sneak attacks; her fiancé's arm was lame, and James was gloating with the fact.

Her fiancé's fist shot blindingly towards James' throat, but James was quick in seizing the wrist of that fist, halting the blow shy of where it was meant to connect. The blow, she understood, would have been fatal had it landed. The fact wasn't lost on James either, for he was suddenly furious. Her fiancé was snatched down, tossed over, and pinned to the floor as a result.

"How about I administer to you a manual version of the same treatment," James growled, hand clasping her fiancé's throat.

Ashley knew fear for her fiancé and herself as well. James wouldn't just choke him unconscious; he'd make it permanent. It would be foolish for him to do otherwise, and in that sense she knew he was anything but foolish. With that, there was absolutely no question of her own demise once he was done with him. Even if he'd had no intention of killing her before, he most certainly would now. She fought down panic, looking from the discarded knife at James' side to the opened door. The knife was within his reach, and she wouldn't make it past him to the door undetected.

She could take a chance and make a daring escape, however, but she couldn't just run out and leave her fiancé. She had to figure a way to save them both. After all, hadn't he come for her? She considered the knife but it was at his side and she would have to venture near in order to retrieve it.

By whatever means, if she were able to grasp it ahead of him, he would then be aware and the element of surprise would be lost. She hadn't been successful earlier in stealing him with the knife, so there was no way she could possibly beat him in a straight forward confrontation with such a primitive weapon. Time was short, running out for the both of them; her fiancé was no longer putting forth a fight…

It occurred to her if he'd known where to find her, wouldn't he also know not to come empty handed? A quick survey revealed an old revolver near the bed. With that, she deduced the preceding. Her fiancé, having busted in the door, had made the costly mistake of getting too close in forcing James away from her, providing the man with an opportunity to snatch up the knife and make use of it. Her fiancé had fumbled the gun.

Ashley slipped quietly from the bed and retrieved the revolver. Her movement was sleight, having gone un-noticed by James. His back was to her as he continued choking her fiancé. It had either happened the way she'd figured it had, or her fiancé's rescue attempt and the gun in her hand were all figments of her imagination, a wishful longing in her dying consciousness. Given the circumstances and the probability of him knowing where, when, and how to find her, she would definitely concede that such was a dying woman's wishful longing, or she was dead already and this was a version of hell, for no part of heaven would be so cruel.

Whether dream, reality, or hell, the object of her torment was at last vulnerable to her deadly attack. The moment she'd been awaiting was upon her. She had to act. She would make no mistake and would give no warning. Her fiancé had nearly cost them their lives with that. It wouldn't be so with her. Besides, she owed him neither warning nor a chance to walk free. She'd sworn revenge. She owed him death and was now in position to deliver.

Ashley gripped the revolver accordingly and aimed. She would empty every round into his head, neck, and back; cold-blooded murder in the first degree. She was an attorney and well acquainted with the law. What with the circumstances– those which she would play heavy upon– she wouldn't see a day behind bars. In the eyes of the law his murder would be justified. She pulled back the hammer. It clicked audibly in the silence, locking in place and awaiting the firing command of her finger on the trigger.

James stiffened.

And in the eyes of the Lord?

The question came unbidden, halting her pull on the trigger. Introduced at first by her fiancé, she knew the Lord's word and had come to trust in it faithfully.

She'd given up on God in recent months, for God had given up on her. Day after day she'd prayed for deliverance and had received everything but. Day after day she'd awakened to various degrees of torment and torture. With every incident she'd grown more bitter with God, wondering how it was that he had forsaken one of his own.

In the eyes of the Lord, it would be cold-blooded murder; she would burn in Hell. But there was no God, right? Neither Heaven nor Hell, so did it matter?

James, trying her with his move, reached out and seized the knife, rising slow to his feet. Again she fingered the cool metal of the trigger. Only a few pounds of pressure and a bullet to the head would drop him forever. No one would ever be threatened nor hurt by him again. James turned to face her, stepping over her fiancé's still figure. Her finger tightened on the trigger.

How then do you hold in your hand the key to freedom? By what miracle had it been provided? By whom then but God?

The revelation was daunting. Her heart beat faster and she knew fear for her negligence of God. Her hand trembled, for never in life had she'd been more convinced of God's existence. With that, she could not murder the man in cold blood. In fact, the desire to do so was suddenly absent. The revelation served to complicate matters in that she would have to warn James off with threats and no serious action.

"I see that your hand trembles," James said. "Are you afraid now, Ashley? It is perfectly understandable, however, considering how the gun you hold is old and rusted. You will find–" he gestured with the knife at her fiancé "–as did this gentleman, the weapon you hold is dysfunctional. Were the situation in reverse I, too, would know your fear."

Dysfunctional gun? Is that how he'd gotten the drop on her fiancé? It made sense. Whereas the revelation of God had shaken her moments ago, she trembled now at James' proclamation. "You're lying," she said, silently praying her words were true.

"Of course you speak only what you wish," he continued. "But that, too, is understandable. The bullets in that gun are old; the explosive compression is little to none. If you pull that trigger there will be little more than a weak poof, and the round will expel no farther than a few feet from the barrel before dropping to the floor. This is what transpired when–" he gestured again at her fiancé "–the gentleman, here, burst in with demands to which I refuse to adhere. I was truly angry with you, Ashley. Even at the threat of gunfire I would not relinquish my hold to your throat. As a result, I would have been dead if the bullets in that gun were not the duds they are."

His boyish face of innocence contorted into one of rage. "The son of a bitch took a shot at me!" he shouted and turned to deliver a kick to her fiancé's torso, facing her again, his features calm, the boyish innocence having returned.

"Ashley," he went on, his voice softer now. "You know how angry I become when defied with futile attacks. You came marginally close with the knife.

I didn't take kindly to it. My intent had been to kill you for that, but, as you can see, I was rudely interrupted. That is fortunate for the both of us; you are alive, and I still have you.

"I love you, Ashley, and I want to have you with me. I want to treat you the way you ought to be treated. I simply need to know that I can trust you. I will forgive and forget your attempt tonight if you would but show you wish me no harm. If you pull that trigger two things will happen: the gun will fire incorrectly, and I will know your intent." James took a single step forward.

Heart racing, thoughts a raging storm of panic, Ashley retreated a step backwards.

"However," James continued. "I will be furious, as you well know, and very much unforgiving in regards to the matter. I will, at that point, remorselessly resume what the gentleman interrupted. On the other hand, if you turn over your weapon, it will serve as a token of trust. It will erase all discrepancy and doubt. My trust in you will be complete. We can—" he gestured around the room and at the still figure of her fiancé "–clean all of this up and move on."

James took a second step, and so did Ashley retreat. He advanced further, and Ashley, close again to retreating, held her ground. He was bluffing about the gun and testing her with his advance, but he had made a critical mistake. His steps were tentative and unsure. She knew him well. If the bullets were the duds he claimed they were, he would be more confident in his approach. No doubt he was praying she didn't pull the trigger.

Ashley tightened her grip on the gun and steadied her aim at James' chest. "Don't come any closer," she said, holding his gaze.

James, midways into a fourth step, drew up short.

"I have nothing to lose, James," she told him. "I simply refuse to believe you would hold true to all you say. Even if you spoke truthfully, I don't accept. I want out, James. This ends tonight. True, I have no knowledge as to the gun's functionality, but it's only fair I make clear my intent to pull the trigger if you so much as step further in my direction." She paused, then added menacingly, "You will truly know my intent then. With that, I'm willing to bet you will also know what a .38 round feels like in your chest."

James' face contorted into a mask of fury, and Ashley, unafraid for the first time in the face of his anger, knew relief. The mere fact he remained in place and did not attack exposed his words for the bluff they were.

James threw back his head and laughed hard, and Ashley was puzzled by it, her certainty wavering. "Okay," James sobered. "Deflating your false sense of security will be pleasant indeed. The chastisement thereafter will be unmerciful. I've given you a chance– your only chance –to redeem yourself, to accept my words on faith. Now that you have chosen, pay close attention and listen, dear Ashley, and I will show you the facts.

Your fiancé kicked in the door and stood there." He pointed to one side and she glanced briefly to where he indicated. "He then moved a few paces over there," James continued and pointed to yet another area to where Ashley glanced. "He commanded me to unhand you, and, as I mentioned before, I refused. His response was an attempt on my life. He pulled back the hammer, and I watched his finger squeezed that trigger.

"I was staring down the barrel so I knew his aim was for my head. He was furious. The barrel emitted a weak explosion– if you can even call it an explosion. The round was meant to punch through my cranium, but it came forth at such a pitiful rate that it traversed approximately three feet and fell to the carpet–" he pointed– "there behind where you stand."

Ashley turned and knew it was a costly error. She faced forward to find James barreling down on her. She recoiled, stumbling backwards in her haste to retreat. James descended upon her and together they fell: James with the knife above head poised to strike, Ashley with the barrel pressed against his chest.

Ashley hesitated in their descent. Once again he was forcing her to choose between life and death, her life or his. The situation was more pressing now than before, and still she hesitated, reluctant to pull the trigger, unwilling to end his life. The deciding factor was the murderous look in his eyes and the fact the blade descended toward her face at a faster rate than which they fell. He was pressing her and she couldn't remain passive and allow him to kill her off.

Ashley pulled twice on the trigger. The explosions were loud. The gun bucked powerfully in her hand, putting to rest any question of the weapons functionality. James' eyes registered shock, pain, and disbelief, which was followed by the abrupt blankness that was death. Ashley's head hit the floor hard. Her vision flashed streaks of blue before dissipating into pixels of black. Her breath escaped fast from her lungs under James dead weight, and the knife fell from his lifeless fingers to land near her head. She filled her lungs deep and willed her vision to clear. She lay panting a second before sliding out from under the dead weight of her antagonist, crawling over to the still figure of her fiancé.

Chapter 20

Trayon opened his eyes to darkness and found himself neither standing, laying, nor sitting, but suspended in space. He suffered a vision of fire, a sensation of falling, a moment's fear– and suddenly all was clear. He remembered the vision's portrayal of Ashley's betrayal, and his distress. He recalled crashing his bike, speaking with God, and falling to the depths of Hell. Only now did he realize he'd been given a second chance to set his heart right with God, to choose correct. It wasn't just his career, well-being, sanity, and his physical health that had depended upon his course of action, but his soul as well– and he had failed miserably.

Clear was the revelation of Ashley's fate and his unsuccessful attempt to rescue her from it. Trayon sighed in the darkness, though there was air to neither breath nor exhale. Once again he knew fear and the sense of doom. For him there would be no tunnel of light to the world beyond. No Heaven or Paradise, or whatever the synonymous term for God's abode. He would know Hell for his failure; eternally acquainted with what he'd only glimpsed before. He recalled his last encounter with death, the darkness parting to reveal what he'd first taken to be a red sea before he'd identified its true nature of fire, the countless wailing of tormented souls rising from its depths.

Trayon's fear intensified, but he did not panic. It would change nothing. God had shown Ashley's infidelity and peril, providing him with adequate means to assist, but he had chosen not to act, condemning himself as a result. God had pointed the err of his ways and had given him a second chance. He couldn't appeal to God for mercy, for death was too late and only actions in life could dictate his fate. He would have to accept life's retribution.

Shame accommodated his fear; a sense of having disappointed God himself, of having disobeyed a direct command from his Father. He had been stubbornly prideful and unforgiving. The thought of having to live with that, to burn for all eternity bearing the shame of such, was daunting. That alone is Hell. So great was his shame he couldn't bear the thought of facing God. He had no desire to plead his case. It would be a reprieve to forgo the encounter and to be cast into the fire. The fact he felt such said more than words for his humility. Besides, God knew the truth in the matter, so what could he possibly say? That he had tried?

"And is that not the truth, my son?" came a voice so powerful it could belong to none other than

God. It emanated from everywhere all at once. *"It is your intent and effort which matters. Your change of heart and decision to forgive has earned you life and grace with me. You've done well, my son. Return and be fruitful."*

Trayon was momentarily disoriented then acutely aware of the physical, that he was on his back and on the surface of something uncomfortable. A searing pain in the pit of his arm echoed a dull ache in his right leg. He knew from where each had derived. There was an abrupt constriction above the wound in his leg, and he cracked open his eyes to spy Ashley working to knot a torn strip of sheet about his thigh in a frantic attempt to stanch the bleeding.

"I'm sorry, baby," Ashley said, unaware she was observed. "This is all my fault. I just needed to be certain. I'm sorry. I never meant to hurt you. I never meant for any of this to happen. Please forgive me. Will you ever forgive me?"

Her obvious distress tore at his heart. He'd coveted those words months before. Now, however, her plea wasn't necessary. He caught her wrist, and her gaze flew to his face. The relief, love, and reverence upon her features were unmistakable.

"I wouldn't be here otherwise," he said. "However, it is I who must beg for your forgiveness." Ashley slid closer and Trayon reached to caress her cheek, sliding his hand to the back of her neck. "I love you, Ashley," he told her. "Always have and always will."

He urged her down to him, and she came willingly, understanding his silent request. Their lips met and they kissed passionately, a tender caressing of tongues implicit of many promises to come. He envisioned them in their flight through the snow covered mountain forest as wolves, him launching after her in open sky, their transformation to multicolored dragons; extraordinary creatures that mated for life.

Coming Soon

Retribution

(Excerpt)

Thomas Habersham

The night was warm, quiet for the most part. Other than an occasional breeze that rustled the leaves above and those on the ground below, nothing moved except a lone figure in black who crept through the backyard gate of a three-bedroom home. Crouching low, the figure kept to the shadows in making its way to the back porch. It pulled a key from under a flower pot, opened the door and crept silently inside.

The intruder stood fast, its eyes adjusting to the gloom. It knew the home's layout as well as the number of individuals who lived here. Children were amongst that number, and the intruder couldn't risk stumbling over abandoned toys and revealing its presence. With that, it tiptoed through the kitchen and cautiously down the hall where it came upon an open bedroom door. A nightlight illuminated the sleeping faces of identical twins. At five years of age, the girls' resemblance to their father was startling. The intruder knew sympathy at their coming loss, breathing a mournful sigh before closing the door quietly and creeping down the hall.

The second door was shut, and with a cautious turn of the doorknob, the intruder paused- listening for sounds of alarm as the bolt broke free of the jamb– then entered soundlessly, alone with the sleeping target....

You never think it will happen to you, that it will land on your doorstep– until it does. Now you can't believe it. Columnist, Dorothy Legler, has drawn the eyes of a deadly kidnapper. A terrifying world unfolds as people she knows turn up missing and those around her have questionable motives. With daring taunts and bold kidnappings, the stalker plays cat and mouse with Topeka Police.

When an officer disappears in the line of duty, and the Feds arrive with lead agent "Hound Dog" Rawls, it's clear Dorothy is Key to one, Target to the other, and the authorities are up against a criminal who is just as deadly as he is cunning. How many victims will be taken before the kidnapper is stopped? Will he be stopped? Or will he snatch the Target before the "Hound" has a chance to unlock his identity?

Order at: www.amazon.com

Kassidy is released after a year in juvenile, but he is welcomed home with violence and war. When one of his best friends is gunned down right in front of him, it is up to Kassidy and his street gang to find out who did it and why.

As Kassidy's rap career rises to new heights, the structure of people built around him screams success—until his past resurfaces during his first performance, forcing another change.

Follow the story of a teenager as he wades through a web of violence, heartbreak, and disloyalty in search of love, revenge, and justice. The conflict here is as strong as the twists are sharp!

Order at: www.amazon.com

CIRCLE OF DEATH

CONFESSIONS OF A BLACK WOMAN

THOMAS HABERSHAM

Infected with a deadly virus, blood on her hands, Alez wreaks havoc on the world around her, bypassing barriers of protection to bring death to one victim after another even as she struggles to cope with isolation and her very own sentence of death.

The rampage falters at her encounter with Kevin, an enigmatic male whose disposition renders him impervious to her methods. Her renewed efforts are balked when the tables are turned. Emotionally attached, Alez must now protect Kevin and keep him oblivious to her deadly secret, both of which become increasingly difficult with every passing moment...

Order at: www.amazon.com